Love Is Everything

A novella by

Elsie Hillman-Gordon

ISBN: 1496112458
ISBN 13: 9781496112453
Library of Congress Control Number: 2014904233
CreateSpace Independent Publishing Platform
North Charleston, South Carolina

Dedication

I dedicate this book to my late parents, Milton and Mary Elizabeth Hillman, the first two people to love me unconditionally and encourage me to dream. Their loving spirits live on through me, their sons, grandchildren, and great-grandchildren.

Acknowledgments

It is wonderful to dream and to have your dreams come true. Writing and publishing this story is one of my dreams, and it has been a labor of love.

I first praise God, my heavenly Father, from whom my blessings flow. I thank him for the creative gift of storytelling. I thank him for planting the story line and characters in my heart and for inspiring me to share this story with others.

I thank my husband, Victor Gordon, for his encouragement and for providing nourishing snacks to me while I spent many hours hunched over my computer, breathing life into my characters.

Thanks to Mary Baker-Brown, Kecia Campbell, Dolores Kinney, and Sharon Willis for listening to me read select chapters, for asking thought-provoking questions, and for simply cheering me on to the finish line.

And thanks very much to *you* for your support. I hope that within these pages you will find something to smile, rejoice, and wonder about.

Always remember that love is everything!

Chapter 1

Soft morning light streamed through the windows, affirming the start of a new September day. It was a welcoming but late affirmation for Vanessa Dennison, who had already been up for a full hour. Wrapped in a cotton robe and sipping a cup of hot tea, Vanessa stared blankly out the window of her spacious suite on the fifty-second floor of the Millennium Hotel in Manhattan. She had going home on her mind. Despite the tempting hotel perks of in-room dining and housekeeping—not to mention a superb panoramic view of the city—she missed her cozy home in Washington, DC. In truth, she missed a lot of things.

There had once been a time when Vanessa relished trips to New York. But that was then, not now. This week, all she had enjoyed was counting down the days until the end of the convention that had brought her to the city in the first place.

As a corporate event planner, Vanessa was managing an A-list client's annual event at the convention center. Aided by a small team of assistants, her duties included overseeing registration and all preparations for receptions, luncheons, award ceremonies, and workshops. She was also the point person for exhibitors and speakers. Now it was the final day of the convention, and she was physically and mentally drained. Her responsibilities had kept her in high gear all week, but even more exhausting was her struggle with the bittersweet memories that had completely dampened her spirit all week.

Since Vanessa's arrival in New York seven days ago, thoughts of her parents had consumed her at every turn. Frank and Gloria Dennison were always near in thought but were relentlessly so this week. Manhattan had been a treasured vacation spot they had shared, and being here without them had opened a floodgate of memories that had nearly overcome her.

The first time her parents brought her to the Big Apple, Vanessa was just five years old. They had traveled by train from their home in Richmond, Virginia, to holiday shop and to see the Radio City Christmas Spectacular. Riding through Central Park in a horse-drawn carriage was a thrill, and it became one of Vanessa's favorite pleasures. Over the decades, as she blossomed from a pretty child into a beautiful woman with a busy life of her own, she and her parents had kept their annual New York adventure alive. Together, they explored and enjoyed Manhattan's legendary neighborhoods of Chinatown, Greenwich Village, Harlem, and Soho. They browsed shops, galleries, and museums; dined at fine restaurants and trendy cafes; and energized their spirits at jazz clubs and Broadway productions. To them, New York was a special annual tradition to continue for many more years to come.

But fate had other plans.

One rainy Saturday night, eighteen months ago, on their way home from visiting a friend, Frank and Gloria were stopped at a red light when a drunk driver plowed his speeding truck, across the rain-slicked road, into their car. The police had been in hot pursuit of the man for several miles. Witnesses had likened the police chase and subsequent crash to a scene straight out of a Hollywood action movie. Only this time there had been no happy ending. Frank and Gloria were instantly killed, and the drunk driver died two days later.

Now, turning away from the window, Vanessa placed her cup on the dining room table next to her breakfast tray. Staring at a plate of toast, potatoes, scrambled eggs, and turkey sausage, a slight frown creased her brow as she thought about the couple of pounds she had gained this week. Between dual pressures of managing the work and her poignant memories, she had given into emotional eating. But she was not overly concerned. Vanessa knew she would burn the pounds off quickly when she was back at her home and into her exercise routines of jogging and bike riding. At five feet six, she strived to maintain her weight around 130 pounds. She appreciated her curves and didn't understand most people's obsession to be extremely thin.

As Vanessa pulled out a chair to sit down at the table, the loud shrill of the hotel phone startled her. Glancing apprehensively at the ringing phone, she breathed deeply to collect herself. Since her parents' accident, late night and early morning phone calls rattled her nerves. On the second ring, she scooted quickly around the chair to answer the call, all the while wondering who it was—and hoping it was her best friend, Rita.

Vanessa met Rita Baxter eighteen years ago during freshmen orientation at Howard University. Sidekicks immediately, they bonded even more after pledging the same sorority. After graduation, Vanessa stayed in DC and pursued an MBA at Georgetown University. Rita moved to Manhattan to work for a small advertising company, where she still worked today but in a senior executive position.

In spite of not living in the same city—Rita lived in Harlem with her boyfriend, Mike Harris—they were still best friends, texting and talking constantly, meeting for marathon shopping at outlets between New York and DC, and rooming together at their sorority's annual conference. They were there for each other through the good and bad times in their lives. Earlier in the week, they had met for dinner and had plans to see a Broadway play later that evening.

Lifting the receiver of the phone, Vanessa hesitated. "Hello?"

"Good morning, Sis. I hope I'm not waking you."

Grateful to hear Rita's voice, Vanessa smiled and replied, "No, you're not. I've been up for a while, anxious to get this last convention day on the road. I'm just relieved it's you and not one of my assistants. It's way too early in the morning to start putting out convention fires."

"You know you can handle any fire blazing in your path."

Vanessa's smile grew. "I didn't say I couldn't handle a fire. It's just too early for one to be crackling. So why are you calling me on this number and not my cell phone?"

"I tried your cell, but I keep getting your voice mail."

"Oh, that's right," Vanessa said, snapping her fingers. "I forgot I'd turned it off last night."

"So how's the convention been going? You seemed to have a tight rein on things when I saw you at dinner on Tuesday."

"All's well in Convention Land, but, then, I don't know how it couldn't be! I drive myself and my team crazy with all the triple-checking of details."

"And that, my sister, is why they pay you very well for the work you do."

Vanessa rolled her eyes and said, "Yeah, well, that's debatable considering the aggravation. Take last night for instance, the sound system died during rehearsal for today's closing concert and I had to round up the engineering team. They worked late, supposedly fixing it, but I'm still nervous that it'll crash again."

"Come on, you know you can't be held responsible for every glitch, right?"

"I know it, but that doesn't stop me from worrying about it."

"And if the sun doesn't shine all day today, are you going to worry about that, too?"

"Ouch! No need to poke me!" Vanessa smiled.

"Yeah, well, you need poking sometimes. You need to learn how to relax— but you will this evening!"

Vanessa ignored her friend's assessment. "So, do you want to have dinner before or after the play?"

"Well, actually, that's why I'm calling you so early." Rita was silent for a moment before continuing, "I have to cancel. I won't be able to go."

Vanessa frowned. "Cancel? What are you talking about?"

"I signed a big client yesterday, and I've got a late afternoon team meeting that I know will run long into the evening. I didn't get home last night until almost 10 p.m."

"Well, congratulations on your new client, but do you really have to cancel? Do I need to remind you how much those theater tickets cost?"

"No, I don't need a reminder about how much I paid for an orchestra seat to the best play in town. But it's cool, because my money's not going to waste."

"And how is that?"

"Well, first, promise me that you won't get mad."

"Mad?" Vanessa asked, suspiciously. "Why should I be mad?"

Rita took a deep breath and plunged in. "Well, once I knew I couldn't make the play, Mike suggested we offer my ticket to his fraternity brother—Elliott— who's in town on business. So last night Mike asked if he wouldn't mind going with you in my place and he agreed." She paused, waiting for a reaction from Vanessa. Receiving none, she continued, encouraged. "In fact, he offered to buy you dinner tonight, if you like!"

Vanessa's heart sank. "Rita, please tell me this is a joke."

"I assure you this is not a joke. Elliott Reeves is a handsome brother and a successful attorney. In fact, he's a senior partner at his firm. Anyway, he's happy to *hang out* with you tonight."

"Hang out with me?" Vanessa sputtered. "Well, that's not going to happen!"

Rita exhaled in frustration. "Why not?"

Wound up now, Vanessa gave her a list. "First of all, I don't need to be fixed up on a blind date—I'm not some homely, desperate chick! Second, you should have talked with me before you and Mike put this little plan in motion. Third, there are too many crazies walking around loose, and being an attorney doesn't mean this guy isn't one of them!"

"Girl, I've met Elliott and I can assure you he's of sound mind!" Then, to break the tension with some humor, she added with a chuckle, "You know, I've warned you about watching all of those victim movies on cable and those old *Law and Order* marathons you're hooked on. Not everybody is a whack job out to get—"

Vanessa cut her off and said, "You can skip the jokes, Rita, because I'm not laughing. I can't get over the fact that you didn't talk with me first."

"Would you have agreed if I'd asked you beforehand?" Rita challenged.

"What do you think?" Vanessa retorted, testily.

"Look, I don't think you really want to get me started on what I think because we would be on this phone for the next hour."

"And what's that supposed to mean?"

"It means you need to take some of that energy you throw into your work and throw it into your social life!" Rita blurted. "Since you broke off your engagement with Craig, I haven't heard you mention one thing about dating. Aren't you tired of being alone?"

Stung, Vanessa snapped back. "What's wrong with being alone? Everybody should try it from time to time. And if you're not careful and keep nagging Mike to marry you when it's clear he doesn't want to, that's just what you're going to be!"

Rita felt her blood pressure rise. *Oh no, she didn't say that,* she thought. *That's a low blow, but I guess I deserve it since I struck first.*

"Okay, okay, let's slow this conversation down," Rita said. She had expected some resistance, but had made the situation far worse with her thoughtless attack on Vanessa's social life. After a long pause, she continued, "Come on, please don't be mad. I'm really sorry—not to mention extremely cranky—from going to bed late last night and getting up too early this morning."

"That makes two of us," Vanessa said, stiffly.

"Sis, you should know my heart. You know my intentions are good. Trust me. I know how hard this week has been for you. Since I can't make it tonight, Mike and I just thought it would be nice if you enjoyed yourself—and Elliott's a great guy. Plus, he lives in DC!"

DC? Vanessa groaned inwardly. *This conversation just keeps getting worse!*

With time ticking and not wanting to spend another minute of it arguing, Vanessa relented. "Look, Rita, if that's your way of apologizing for not inviting me to have a say in who I spend my time with, well, I guess I'll accept it for the sake of our friendship," she said flatly. "In the meantime, I've got a lot of work to focus on today, and I've got to hang up and get organized. I'll text you later and let you know what I plan to do about tonight."

"Well, I kind of need to know now," Rita pressed. "Mike needs to tell Elliott something."

"You know *exactly* what he can tell him!" Vanessa said hotly. Her biting tone made Rita think of those feisty "housewife" characters on TV with their hands on their hips, eyes rolling, and threatening to give somebody a serious beat down. Trying to imagine Vanessa in that role made Rita laugh, and the sound she made when she laughed was hilarious in itself. It was a laugh that never failed to make Vanessa smile even when she didn't want to—like at this very moment.

Still unhappy, Vanessa exhaled and slowly surrendered to one of those exasperating "whatever" moments in life. After a few moments, she agreed to meet Elliott but passed on his dinner invitation. Rita thought of asking her to reconsider dinner but held back fearing another argument.

Finally, their spirited conversation ended with a promise to talk later. Hanging up the phone, Vanessa gently massaged her temples, feeling a headache coming on. *A blind date,* she thought grimly. *After the week I've had, that's the last thing I need!*

Moments later, after taking two aspirin, she walked deliberately over to the desk in the bedroom and lifted the lid on her laptop computer. A few clicks of the keyboard landed her on the website for United Airlines. *I wonder how much they'd charge to change my departure from tomorrow morning to a flight later this evening.*

Chapter 2

In Vanessa's hotel room, the windows were now filled with sunshine as she sat fully dressed at the table, reviewing today's convention schedule. Her uneaten breakfast had been pushed aside, as had any remaining negative thoughts about Mike and Rita. Instead she focused on what was most important at the moment—wrapping up the final key events on this last day of the convention.

The first thing on Vanessa's schedule was a meeting in an hour with Steve Lawrence, the association's executive director. Steve, a silver-haired man with a kind disposition, was the first to interview her for the convention manager consultant position. At the end of the competitive process, she had been selected over four other consultants. Within a short period of time, Steve had become her number one cheerleader, supporting her contract recommendations, new vendor selections, and giving her the liberty to make changes to the existing lineup of concurrent sessions and all-day workshops.

Time to get this day going, Vanessa thought. Snapping her agenda closed, she stood up and walked to the mirror to check her appearance. She was wearing a stylish, navy pantsuit and a pair of comfortable flats in the exact color of her suit. A navy, red, and white silk scarf was casually draped around her neck. Satisfied with her reflection in the mirror, she gathered her bags, grabbed her sweater from the closet, and left the suite.

Three hours later, Vanessa walked along the carpeted path in the exhibit hall for one final look around. But she wasn't the only one doing the looking. With her long, dark brown hair, gorgeous almond-shaped brown eyes, and soft, caramel skin tone, she attracted the attention of practically everyone on her path.

Earlier in the week, a man had stopped her in the exhibit hall and said, "You look like that beautiful black actress in that movie starring what's-his-name." Vanessa had smiled politely but kept moving, not bothering to help the man figure out the actress, the movie, or what's-his name.

Strolling along the corridors, Vanessa's thoughts drifted back to just a few days ago when she had been in awe of the energy in this hall. Thousands of people had tightly crammed the aisles to purchase and sell high-tech equipment. There were also technology and education areas for interactive exhibits and live demonstrations. But now, with only several hours remaining before the official close of the convention, there were only a couple of hundred registrants on the exhibit floor, many of whom were walking the aisles looking for whatever was left of the free giveaways. Many exhibitors were slowly dismantling their booths and packing up their expensive, high-tech equipment and other valuable merchandise.

With her head down fiddling with papers in her hand, Vanessa quickly turned the corner and just barely missed bumping hard into a man who, like her, was blindly turning the corner. Their near-miss collision caused her to lose her balance, sending the papers in her hands tumbling to the floor. As she stumbled, he reached his arms out and caught her, bringing her to a safe upright position.

Embarrassed at her clumsiness, Vanessa smiled weakly at him and said, "Excuse me. My mind was somewhere else."

"No, it's my fault for not paying attention. Here, let me get those papers you dropped," he said, leaning over and picking them up.

Vanessa stepped back to get a better look at the handsome man with the chocolate-brown complexion—who had almost knocked her off her feet. At six feet tall with a muscular build, he was wearing a black suit, and a white open-collared dress shirt.

"Are you okay?" he asked, handing her the papers.

"I'm fine," she said with a smile.

"I'm glad to hear it. I couldn't forgive myself if you had fallen." Studying her face for a moment, he continued, "I saw you pass through here a couple of days ago, looking like someone in charge of things. I was hoping for a chance to say hello—although not by knocking you over!"

Pleasantly surprised by his observations, Vanessa looked at the man curiously. He was intriguing—polite, well-dressed, and definitely charming. She found her eyes shifting to his left hand to see if he was wearing a wedding band. He was not.

"Are you one of our exhibitors this year?" she asked.

"No, I'm not an exhibitor. Actually, I'm here to—"

Suddenly, a loud, musical sound invaded their space. It was her cell phone's ringtone. Annoyed by the interruption of a call at this very moment, Vanessa thought, *I wish I had kept this thing turned off!* Quickly pulling it from her bag, she checked the caller ID screen and saw that it was the association's CEO. Vanessa looked up into the warm brown eyes of the man who had caught her from falling and smiled. "Excuse me, but I really have to take this call."

"Sure, I understand," he said cordially but with a hint of disappointment. "I need to be on my way, but promise me you'll be careful turning these corners."

"You have my word, no more mishaps today," she laughed, raising her voice slightly to compensate for the insistent ringing. Then, with a reluctant parting smile, she looked at her phone and pushed the talk button. "Yes, Margaret, how can I help you?" she asked as she walked toward the exit.

Reaching the door at the end of the hallway, Vanessa paused from talking and glanced back to see if she could spot the handsome stranger. To her surprise, he was standing right where she'd left him, his eyes locked on her. *Mister, you are making my day!* she thought. Then, turning around, she pushed the metal door open and walked through it.

Seated at a desk in a large office in the convention center, Vanessa looked out at a crowd of people networking and sharing industry news and gossip. The first set of concurrent sessions had ended with the final round about to begin in ten minutes. Her team was out and about, changing signs outside the meeting rooms and checking audiovisual requirements.

Dennis Wilson, one of five association staff members assigned to assist Vanessa, sat on the carpeted floor adjacent to her desk, packing up several large boxes of office supplies and other materials to ship back to the association's office in DC.

"So, Vanessa, this is it—the last day!" Dennis said. He paused and looked up at her.

"Yes, it is," she said, without looking at him.

Coming aboard as a consultant to lead an existing convention team had not been particularly easy for Vanessa, and Dennis had been a real menace. He had been, and presumably still was, a good friend of the previous manager who was terminated for badly negotiating several vendor and hotel contracts. From the beginning, Dennis had tried to undermine Vanessa by aggressively challenging and knocking some of the new ideas that she brought forth. Vanessa welcomed team input but not disrespectful behavior. She had pulled Dennis aside and warned him that she'd dismiss him from her team, if it happened again. The thought of being left behind to manage the phones while his colleagues enjoyed the perks of business travel had been enough to adjust his disposition. Since then he'd tried being friendly, but she had kept him at a distance.

Gazing into the crowd outside the door, Vanessa spotted Steve standing with a couple of the association's board members. Their morning meeting had gone extremely well with Steve talking enthusiastically about certain areas of the convention in which he believed she had made a significant difference. He had even gone so far as to credit her with increased attendance due to a fresh lineup of several new session topics she had suggested they produce. In wrapping up the meeting, he had asked if she would be interested in the permanent position of convention manager. Flattered by the offer, she knew she would not take it because her consulting work offered her the two things she craved—variety in work and flexibility in schedule. But instead of flatly turning down the offer, she told him that she'd mull it over and give him an answer next week.

"It's been a great convention," Dennis said. "I bet Steve is pleased, huh?"

Vanessa gave him a sideways glance. "You can ask him yourself. I believe he'll be here in a minute," she said as she stood, preparing to leave the office. "I have a quick meeting before the closing luncheon. If you need to reach me before I see you and the rest of the team at lunch, you have my cell number."

And with that, Vanessa was off to her meeting with Margaret Richardson, the caller who had interrupted her conversation with the handsome man in the exhibit area. Margaret sat on the board of two nonprofits based in DC and had asked Vanessa to stop by the association's hospitality suite to discuss a possible event-planning opportunity with one of the nonprofits. Vanessa was happy for the meeting—and the opportunity it offered to continue growing her consulting business.

Chapter 3

It was 5 p.m. when Vanessa unlocked the door to her hotel suite. As she stepped inside, a wave of relief washed over her. The convention had officially ended a few hours earlier, and on an incredibly high note—thanks to an exhilarating closing concert that had been free of any technical glitches.

Setting her sweater and bags to the side, Vanessa stepped out of the comfortable flats that had served her well all day. She was pleased that the convention had been a success and just as pleased that it was over. As she turned toward the table in the main area, she stopped in her tracks. *Who sent flowers?* The beauty of a dozen yellow roses greeted her. The hotel staff had delivered them while she was out.

Curious, Vanessa walked over for a closer look at the stunning arrangement. A white card, perched among the delicate blossoms and green foliage, read: "Congratulations on a job well done! Love, Uncle Ray and Aunt Rachel." *How sweet! And so like them,* she thought.

It was a sunny, cheerful bouquet, but as Vanessa leaned forward to smell its sweet fragrance, suddenly, memories flashed in her mind of all the flowers that had been delivered to her parents' home in Richmond after the news spread of their accident. So many floral arrangements had arrived that Vanessa had asked family members to deliver them to patients at a nearby hospice. Many of the flowers were sent by people Vanessa had never met—people who had known and loved her parents, the good Drs. Frank and Gloria Dennison.

As her breath caught in her throat, Vanessa grabbed the first diversion she spotted—a glossy visitor's guide to the city—and sat down, determined not to let her thoughts travel back in time. But as she flipped through the pages without seeing them, her determination failed, and a flood of memories poured over her. Tears began slipping down her cheeks, one by one, until she started sobbing, and the guide slipped to the floor.

Vanessa's parents had been an extraordinary couple—highly regarded for their medical expertise, personal accomplishments, and community activities. Married for thirty-seven years, they were still as crazy about each other as the day they'd first met strolling across the campus of Howard University, from where they had both graduated magna cum laude. And together they had loved and spoiled their only daughter, Vanessa.

Fortunately for Vanessa, Frank's eldest brother, Ray, and his wife, Rachel, had been there as a lifeline, seeing her through the most difficult time of her life. Her heart swelled with gratitude to them, for everything they had done— and continued to do—for her. Ray was a Baptist minister who had retired from preaching for health reasons. A wise and patient man, he often reminded Vanessa to give thanks to God—not only for blessing her with amazing parents, but for bestowing on her the wonderful qualities that had made her such a pleasing daughter. After the accident, however, Vanessa had been too angry at God to express gratitude.

Following the funeral service, Vanessa had stayed on in Richmond with her uncle and aunt, conferring with attorneys about her parents' estate and packing up valuable items from the family home that now belonged to her. After a few weeks, her uncle and aunt returned to their home in Newport News, Virginia, and she returned to DC where she moved dazedly about, trying to figure out what to do now that her life had turned upside down.

Many days Vanessa didn't know what to do: stay in bed with the covers over her head, or get up and pretend that she could function after the loss of her parents. Six months prior to the accident, she had launched her consulting career. With project deadlines rapidly approaching and clients calling, somehow she managed to pull herself together by day—pouring all of her energy into her work—only to collapse in tears under the covers at night.

Loud laughter coming from the hotel hallway broke Vanessa's contemplation. Sniffling as she wiped away tears, she got up and turned on the television, inviting conversation into a room that was quiet and lonely. A glance at her watch told her she had several hours before the start of tonight's Broadway play. She was still peeved with Mike and Rita for setting her up on this unwanted date, but she had abandoned the idea of leaving town today. It had been an emotional week; it would be good therapy to relax this evening at the best play on Broadway.

After taking several deep breaths to calm her spirit, Vanessa's time management skills kicked in, and she made a mental checklist of things to do before heading to the theater: call her uncle and aunt to thank them, try to catch a thirty minute nap, take a quick shower, and grab a light bite to eat.

Chapter 4

The evening air in New York City was surprisingly cool for the first week in September. Draping her pink pashmina shawl around her shoulders, Vanessa paused outside her hotel, wondering if she should take a taxi or a brisk walk to the theater district.

Enjoying the cool breeze, Elliott Reeves walked the short distance from the Marriott Hotel to the theater. Turning the corner on West Forty-Sixth Street, he observed a long line of people standing in front of the brightly lit theater for tonight's performance. He glanced at his watch; it was 7:30 p.m. Moving forward to get in line, he noticed dozens of African-American women lined up ahead of him—some with and some without theater companionship. He wondered if one of them might be Rita's friend, Vanessa.

Four hours earlier, Elliott had met Mike at a restaurant in Times Square for a late lunch and to pick up the theater ticket. Rita had told Mike to make the ticket a gift to Elliott because it would be a shame to have him pay to sit next to Vanessa if she showed up with a bad attitude. But Elliott had insisted on paying for the ticket. He was somewhat amused to learn that Rita's friend had turned down his dinner invitation, but he understood. Like her, he was not interested in making a love connection. However, unlike her, he was at least open to the idea of meeting at the theater and engaging in a round of friendly conversation.

Mike had opened up over lunch and shared with Elliott that he and Rita were going through a rocky patch in their relationship. She was pressing him to get married because her biological clock was ticking and she wanted a baby, but he wanted to wait another year on both of those big events. Elliott listened with

interest but wisely gave the only advice he knew how to give: be totally honest—and the sooner the better. He also reminded Mike that fatherhood was a
serious, fulltime, and long-term responsibility. His friend listened, appreciating
the sound advice he knew he could count on from Elliott.

Mike and Elliott had met several years ago seated next to each other at
a New York Knicks game at Madison Square Garden. Strangers when the
game began, they were like old buddies by the time it ended. After some good-
naturedly trash-talking of each other's team, their conversation had shifted, and
they had discovered they were both members of the same fraternity. At the end
of the game, they exchanged their contact information and stayed in touch by
phone, sometimes catching a game together when one traveled to the other
one's town. Elliott had talked with Rita over the phone several times, but had
only met her in person once.

Now, inside the crowded theater, Elliott stood in front of his seat, facing the rear of the theater in anticipation of Vanessa's arrival. He wished he
knew a little more about her and what she looked like. When he'd asked Mike
for a general description, he had just smiled and said, "Man, you will not be
disappointed." There were three empty seats in his row. After several minutes,
a well-dressed couple approached and stopped at the end of the row. Smiling
at them, Elliott stepped into the aisle, allowing them easy access to their seats.
Now, there was only one empty seat next to his seat on the aisle and it belonged
to Vanessa.

At 8 p.m. sharp the lights were lowered, taking with it all the noisy chatter. Before taking his seat, Elliott looked toward the rear of the theater one
final time for any sign of the mystery woman approaching. Not seeing anyone
headed his way, he sat down and settled back in his seat. *I guess she's not coming.*
As the stage curtain opened and the orchestra began playing, he turned his full
attention to the stage.

Fifteen minutes later, an usher guided Vanessa to a rear orchestra seat on
the opposite aisle of her ticketed seat assignment. Because she was late arriving,
she would have to wait for the next break in the performance to move to her
assigned seat down front next to Elliott.

By the end of the first act, there was barely a dry eye in the house. The
supporting actor had just finished a dramatic death bed scene. It was a stunning
performance, one that was certain to earn him a Tony nomination. Elliott was

amazed by the acting. Vanessa was not certain which was affecting her emotions more: the story unfolding on stage or the memory of being in this theater with her parents.

When the lights were raised for intermission, a myriad of conversations quickly filled the air. Stepping into the aisle to stretch his legs, Elliott weaved quickly through the crowd and walked to the rear of the theater. Meanwhile, Vanessa stood and made her way to her assigned seat down front.

Glancing through her Playbill program, Vanessa noticed out of the corner of her eye someone standing to the right of her seat. Looking up, her eyes locked on a face she immediately recognized—the man she had nearly bumped into this morning in the exhibit hall. Momentarily confused to see him standing there, she noted that he looked pleasantly surprised. Suddenly things fell in place. *He's my date tonight!*

Elliott smiled generously. "It seems we meet again!" Holding out his hand, he added, "And this time, let me introduce myself before your phone rings. I'm Elliott Reeves. And I assume you're Vanessa—Rita's friend."

"Yes, I'm Vanessa." She smiled back, standing to shake his hand warmly. "And don't worry, my phone is turned off!"

The two laughed, enjoying the strange coincidence that had brought them together.

"I'm glad you're here, but what happened to make you miss the first act?"

"Actually, I only missed the first fifteen minutes. On the way here, I stopped to help an elderly man who fell crossing the street. Since I was late, the usher guided me to an aisle seat near the back to wait for a break in the performance."

"Oh, I see," Elliot said, nodding his head. "Well, I'm glad you're here now."

"That makes both of us!"

"Is the man okay?"

"I hope so—I helped him into a store to sit down. The manager said she'd keep an eye on him and call for help if he needed it."

"Well, that was kind of you to stop and help." Glancing at his watch, Elliott said, "You know, I think we still have a few minutes before intermission is over. Would you like something from the concession stand?"

Vanessa smiled. "Yes, actually, a bottle of water would be great."

"That's all? No snack to go with it?"

"No thanks—but only because I have a cookie tucked in my bag."

Elliott grinned. "Hey, I like the way you think and plan ahead."

"Then you'll also like the fact that it's large enough to share."

"Ha! Even better!" he laughed. He turned to go. "I'll be right back."

"Wait, I'll go with you."

As Vanessa stepped into the aisle to join him, Elliott stole a glance at her. She looked fabulous in a green satin blouse with a sassy-looking black skirt. After seeing her this morning in the exhibit hall, he had thought of her several times throughout the day, inwardly kicking himself for letting her walk away without asking her name or exchanging business cards.

As they started up the aisle, a large group coming in the opposite direction engulfed Vanessa, and she and her date became separated. Elliott quickly maneuvered through the crowd to assist her. Placing his hand lightly at her elbow, he gently guided her through the theatergoers. Vanessa turned and looked at him. "Are you afraid I'm going to almost fall again?" she teased. In reply, Elliott chuckled.

As her date made his purchases at the concession stand, Vanessa stood to the side, waiting. For the second time in one day, she found herself admiring this man. Elliott had an attractive fade haircut and a meticulously trimmed goatee that framed his handsome face perfectly. But it was his eyes—which seemed to look right into her soul—that really engaged her. Removing the wrapper on her big oatmeal cookie, she smiled as he approached with her water.

For several minutes, the two exchanged small talk. Elliott explained that he'd been in town the past few days handling business with a Manhattan law firm. It had turned out that his younger cousin was also in town, managing an exhibitor's booth at the convention. Neither had seen each other in several years so Elliott had stopped by the exhibit hall a few times to talk with him.

"Did your cousin get a lot of visitors at his booth?" Vanessa asked, her event-planning side curious.

"I think he did. He had promotional gifts to give away, and that always draws a crowd." Pausing, Elliott looked directly at Vanessa and continued, "Anyway, while I was in the exhibit hall talking with him, *you* walked right by us."

"Oh, I see." *How in the world did I miss seeing you?*

Just then, a chime sound indicated the end of intermission. Finishing up the cookie they shared, they made their way back down the aisle to their seats.

The second act of the play was as emotional as the first. When Vanessa's eyes filled with tears, she quickly dabbed the corners with a tissue, hoping not to draw Elliott's attention, but it was too late. He had noticed and tilted his head in her direction.

Assuming Vanessa's tears were triggered by the play, Elliott impulsively reached over and placed his left hand gently on top of her right hand. The warm touch of his hand caught her by surprise. She liked it. Suddenly, she was grateful for a dark theater to hide her fickle state of emotions that within seconds had fluctuated from anguish and grief to something she couldn't quite grasp—and didn't necessarily want to believe she was feeling!—about a man who was still very much a stranger. After a couple of minutes, she lightly nodded her head to signal that she was all right, and Elliott removed his hand.

When the play ended an hour later, Elliott suggested they extend the evening and get something to eat. Vanessa readily agreed even though she had rejected the idea to dine with him in her morning conversation with Rita. The big chain restaurants and other popular eateries unique to New York were crowded, and the wait list was long. Eager to sit down and get to know each other, they settled on a modest, less-crowded café.

After a short wait, the hostess ushered them to a table near the window and handed them menus. Elliott quickly made a decision and placed his menu down on the table, while Vanessa took her time looking over the menu, her head lightly swaying to the beat of soft jazz playing in the background. Elliott smiled as he watched her, thinking how surprising it was that he was here with the beautiful woman from the exhibit hall. Things like this only happen in movies and yet—there she was across from him!

The waitress came over, carrying two glasses of water, ready to take their order. Vanessa had decided on the chicken tortilla soup and an iced tea while Elliott ordered fish and chips and a cola.

After the waitress left, Elliott leaned forward and said, "So, Vanessa, here's what I know about you: you live in DC, you're a corporate event planner, and you're Rita's best friend. I want to know more."

"Oh, where do I begin?" Vanessa said, flashing a pretty smile. Sitting back in her chair, she said, "Well, I recently bought a house, so I'm learning how to fix things that look like they're about to fall apart."

Elliott laughed. "Like what, for example?"

"Mainly the appliances—several of them are old and came with the house. I'm going to have to go shopping very soon for a new washing machine and oven." Vanessa paused, noticing that Elliott was listening intently. "I also love movies, books, live theater, and museums. Oh, and according to Rita, I watch way too many reruns of *Law and Order*."

Elliott laughed. "I love *Law and Order* reruns. I can watch them all day!"

"Well, as an attorney, I can understand your interest in the show. But what's my excuse?"

They both laughed.

"So, Elliott, what other things interest you?"

"Actually, some of the same things you mentioned. I enjoy good books, especially mysteries and legal thrillers—also, topics on history and politics. I like movies and documentaries. And I'm a fitness junkie—I like to ride my bike, play tennis, and basketball."

Vanessa smiled. "I like staying fit, too. I ride my bike most weekends."

Elliott nodded his head, appreciating her interest in bike riding.

The waitress arrived with their drinks.

After taking a sip of iced tea, Vanessa played with her straw. "Elliott, do you mind if I ask how old you are?"

Elliott smiled. "Hmmm, why do you ask? Do I look too old to be out with you?"

Vanessa chuckled. "No, not at all—I'm just curious. But if it bothers you, you don't have to tell me."

Elliott held up his hands in a playful gesture of surrender. "No, I don't mind telling you. I recently turned forty-three." He paused and then said, "Now, it's your turn, my friend."

Vanessa smiled. "I'm thirty-five. Thirty-six is breathing down on me hard, but who's counting?"

Elliott grinned as he took a sip of his cola. "Well, certainly not me. I stopped counting birthdays at thirty-nine."

With a smile Vanessa replied, "I hear you. I think that'll be my plan of action, too." After a pause, she asked, "Do you come to Manhattan often?"

"Well, it depends on how you define often. I travel here for business about three times a year, and for pleasure when I want to see a new show on Broadway. What about you?"

"I used to come here quite a bit for pleasure," she began, then said slowly, "but…not so much…lately." Feeling awkward, she looked away, turning her attention toward the window.

Elliott followed Vanessa's gaze onto the crowded streets. Misreading her thoughts, he said, "The view of the city is amazing from the Empire State Building. They offer tours until the wee hours of the morning. If you like, we could go there when we're finished and take a tour."

"That's a really nice idea," she said softly, "but I don't think I'm up to it."

"It's an experience you won't forget!" he coaxed, gently.

Vanessa slowly nodded and turned to face him. "I know," she said quietly. "And that's the problem." Then she briefly explained about her parents' accident and how, over the years, Manhattan with all its venues and attractions and sights—including the spectacular view from the Empire State Building—had come to represent special family time.

When Vanessa was done talking, Elliott's face reflected his sorrow for her. But he looked her squarely in the eye. "I'm so very sorry for your tremendous loss. Being here this week must have been incredibly…*incredibly* difficult for you—and running a convention at the same time." He shook his head, and then simply said, "You must be exhausted."

Blotting her eyes with a napkin, Vanessa agreed with a nod of her head.

After a few quiet moments, Elliott asked softly, "Vanessa, do you believe in God?"

Oh, please, not that question. Vanessa lowered her eyes. With a sigh, she said, "There are days when I don't know what I believe. It's kind of complicated."

"I don't mean to pry. The only reason I asked is because I'd like to say a prayer for you."

Vanessa flinched.

"Is that okay?" he asked gently.

"I don't know—I've been so angry with God," she told him honestly.

She wanted to tell Elliott that she used to be bold in her faith in God. She was baptized at a young age and grew up in the church—singing in the choir, serving as an usher, and working with several outreach ministries. But her faith took flight when her parents died tragically, and she was no longer sure what she believed in anymore.

Vanessa looked back up at Elliott. "But maybe prayer is just what I need."

"Amen," Elliott said, barely above a whisper. Leaning forward, he extended his hands to her, and she reached over and grasped them. He lowered his head, praying softly but fervently. "Almighty God, I'm grateful to you for this day that you have blessed me with. I thank you for bringing a new friend, Vanessa, into my life. God, you know what she is struggling with. Help her to remember that she is never alone, and that you are with her every minute of every day, and all she has to do is believe and trust in your word; a word that assures us there is peaceful rest for all who call on your name. Thank you and Amen."

Elliott gently squeezed her hands, and they sat back as the waitress approached with their entrees. As she topped off their drinks, Vanessa reflected on Elliott's strong faith in God. She found it refreshing to know he felt that way, despite her own uncertainties. When the waitress walked away, Vanessa said, "Thank you for the beautiful prayer, Elliott."

"My pleasure," he replied softly. After a quiet moment, he added, "As you may know, I've also lived through the pain of losing a loved one. Did Rita tell you that my wife died of breast cancer three years ago?"

Vanessa shook her head. "No, she didn't...I had no idea," she fumbled. "Elliott, I don't even know what to say—I'm so sorry!" Tears stung her eyes once again.

"Thanks, Vanessa." Seeing her upset, he said, "Look, I'm sorry to spring that on you; I thought you knew." After a moment, he added, "All I can say is that without a loving God to lean on, and the support of family and friends, I don't know where I'd be today."

Vanessa nodded, regaining her composure. "I'm just a leaky faucet today," she joked, dabbing her eyes.

After a few moments, she asked, "Do you have any children?"

Elliott's expression instantly brightened. "Yes, I do! I have a nine-year-old daughter, Nicole. She's the light of my life!" Pulling his cell phone from the pocket of his jacket, he smiled. "Let me show you her photo." After flipping through a few images, he turned the phone around for Vanessa to view his daughter's picture.

Vanessa studied the cheerful face of the young girl. She had the same warm eyes as her father. "She's very pretty. I imagine her mother's passing was difficult for her."

"Yes, it was difficult, and it still is," Elliott admitted, putting the phone back into his pocket. "As an adult, I know about life and death. I know that good people can die too soon—and bad ones can live too long. I know that life's not fair, and you take the bitter with the sweet and balance it all as best you can. But my daughter is young and not there yet. She misses her mother, so we have our moments of wrestling with grief. But we can't allow ourselves to get lost in it because then we can't move forward."

"Elliott, you have such a healthy perspective on processing grief. I admire it! I'm afraid I've had a hard time focusing on the positive side of grief or death."

"Well, from my perspective, the positive side of death is heaven." Elliott looked at Vanessa, thoughtfully. "From my own experience with grief, this is what I've discovered: when I think less about the physical loss, and more about what I still have—which are my cherished thoughts and feelings for my wife—I don't feel as overwhelmingly sad. But I'll be honest. I didn't get here overnight. It took a long time to reach this point. All I'm saying is that you've got to keep moving forward, putting one foot in front of the other, all the while carrying your loved ones in your heart. Don't block your memories. Embrace them. And keep holding on to God through it all."

Why is that so hard for me? Vanessa thought.

"I don't know if you went through bereavement counseling, but if you didn't and you think you could benefit from it, it's never too late. I can refer you to a counseling group. Talking about your feelings will stir up emotions, but it's therapeutic."

"Thanks, I just might consider it."

The jolting buzz of Elliott's cell phone interrupted their conversation. The incoming text message was from Mike. It read: "Rita and I want to know what's up with you and Vanessa? You two having fun? Did she even show up? (LOL) Hit me back. Mike."

Elliott shook his head and laughed. He turned the phone so Vanessa could read the message. She laughed, too, especially at the part asking if she had shown up. *I bet Rita put him up to that*, she thought.

Elliott gave her a playful wink and said, "Let's just keep the two of them wondering for a while."

She smiled. "You won't get an argument from me!"

And with that, the heavy conversation of grief dissipated. Over the next hour, they sat back and relaxed. They talked about their respective careers, his daughter, and what they liked best and least about living in the nation's capital city.

"Vanessa, this evening has been very special," Elliott said, standing in the lobby of her hotel later that night. "The play was great, but meeting you has been the best part of my entire day!"

Vanessa felt herself blushing. "Thanks, Elliott. I feel the same way about meeting you." Then, thinking about her emotional meltdown over dinner, she added, "And thanks for your thoughtful prayer."

"You're welcome." Pausing a moment, Elliott said, "So, I never asked if you're seeing anyone socially. Are you currently in a relationship?" He hoped she wasn't.

"No, I'm not," she confirmed, quickly adding, "What about you?"

"No, I'm not seriously dating anyone." Elliott smiled warmly at her. "I hope we can get together when we get back to DC. Perhaps dinner and a movie?"

"Dinner and a movie sounds great."

"It's settled then." Elliott paused, looking around at people coming and going in the lobby. "Would you like me to ride up on the elevator with you?"

"Thanks for the offer, but I'll be okay."

Wondering if Vanessa had misconstrued his offer, Elliott tilted his head to the side, so he could look into her eyes. With a wide smile, he said, "Now, don't get me wrong. I'm only talking about providing security to the outside of your room, *and that's all.*"

Vanessa chuckled. "Well, I appreciate you clearing that up. But seriously, I'll be fine."

"I'd feel a whole lot better knowing you got to your room safely. I tell you what—why don't we do this: you have my cell number, so send me a text message to let me know you are safe and sound."

That's sweet, Vanessa thought. *Who is this wonderful man?* "Okay, I'll send you a text message."

Several minutes later, Vanessa exited the elevator and walked quickly toward her corner suite. Once inside, she locked the door and turned on the table lamp. Passing the large mirror hanging on the wall, she stopped and stared at her reflection. She saw something she had not seen in a very long time—a genuine smile of happiness on her face.

Pulling out her cell phone, she punched in Elliott's number and typed a text message: "I'm safe & sound. Thanks for everything! Vanessa."

Standing in the cool night air outside the hotel, Elliott reflected on the captivating Vanessa Dennison. But before he could lose himself any further in his thoughts, his cell phone buzzed. Reading Vanessa's text message, he smiled and replied with his own message: "You're welcome. Have a safe trip home!"

A few seconds later, Elliott's cell phone buzzed again. He looked at the caller ID, hoping it was Vanessa. It was Mike again, determined to get an update. Smiling broadly, Elliott answered the call with a cheerful greeting, "Hey, Mike, what's up?"

Chapter 5

As the airplane taxied down the runway for takeoff, Vanessa sat upright in her seat, staring out the window. Images of Elliott over dinner—his earnest look of concern and sincere prayer to God for her well-being, his head back laughing at her amusing event planning stories, his fingers lightly tapping to soft jazz tunes—filled her mind as it replayed snippets of last night's conversation. She hoped the magnetism she felt between them was real and not imagined.

Minutes later, the airplane ascended, and she took a parting glimpse of the Manhattan skyline, her loving family memories rushed forward. *What was Elliott's advice? "Don't block your memories. Embrace them."* Taking his advice to heart, she laid her head back against the seat and closed her eyes, allowing her thoughts to rush back in time. *Dad loved taking the subway to Harlem in search of soul food, and Mom always had to take a brief stroll through Central Park.* Her good memories flowed freely for a while.

Shortly after, Vanessa's thoughts shifted to the state of her faith in God. She had allowed her grief to cripple her once firm assurance in a heavenly father. She wondered why. So often, grief strengthens a person's faith. Whatever the reason, she knew it was time to renew her belief, because turning her back on a loving God during the worst time of her life had been a mistake that had cost her dearly.

When the plane landed a short time later in DC, Vanessa was deep in prayer. She thanked God for blessing her with parents who had given her so many positive experiences—to grow by, to enjoy in life, and to remember. She smiled as she thought of her uncle and how he would consider her new mindset nothing less than a heavenly breakthrough—a miracle of sorts. And to that, she knew he would simply say, *"To God be the Glory."*

Chapter 6

Vanessa's spirit soared on this sunny Sunday afternoon. She was feeling refreshed. After spending the past week in a hotel, last night she had fallen asleep in her own king-size bed and had slept straight through until 9 a.m.

Seated at the table in her cozy, lemon-colored kitchen, Vanessa was grating sharp cheddar to put in a macaroni and cheese casserole. She had only been home a few hours yesterday afternoon when her next door neighbor, Julie, had stopped by to deliver mail that had come in her absence. On top of the stack was an invitation to a Mary Kay party that Julie was having today. She had been kind enough to collect the mail—and looked so hopeful—that Vanessa found herself agreeing to go.

When Vanessa moved into the neighborhood a year ago, Julie had dropped by the same day with a welcome basket of fruit. Vanessa suspected the basket had mostly been a cover to get inside for a closer look. She had spotted Julie earlier, eyeing her furnishings as the movers unloaded the truck. Since then, the two of them had become good neighbors, keeping a watchful eye on each other's home.

As Vanessa gathered the mustard, milk, and flour for the macaroni, suddenly, her doorbell rang. *Who could that be?* Setting down the ingredients, she moved to the dining room where a side window offered a partial view of her front porch. Peeking through the curtain, she saw a man at her door, holding a vase of pink roses. When he turned in her direction, Vanessa saw his face and jerked away from the window. *Oh, my God!* The last time she had seen Craig Holmes was a year and a half ago—when he was still her fiancé.

Vanessa covered her mouth with her hands. *What's he doing here?* Their relationship had ended badly, and his visit was an unsettling surprise. She didn't dare move, fearing to make a sound. The door bell rang again, followed by soft tapping on her glass storm door. *Just because you're knocking doesn't mean I'm answering!* Vanessa thought.

After a few minutes of silence, a dog began barking, and Vanessa carefully peeked out. Craig was getting into the driver's side of his BMW convertible. He sat in his car, staring at her front door as if willing it to open. After what seemed like an eternity, he finally started the engine and pulled away from the curb.

After Craig drove away, Vanessa moved through the rooms, closing all the blinds a bit more tightly to ensure privacy. Agitated, she finished her casserole preparations, wondering why he had dropped by her home after all this time. *That man's timing has always been off,* she frowned as she placed the dish in the oven and set the timer for thirty minutes. After cleaning off the table, Vanessa hurried upstairs to shower and dress for the party. She was in no mood to go now, thanks to Craig's visit.

Forty minutes later, dressed and ready to go to Julie's house, Vanessa peeked out the window to ensure that Craig had not returned. She was relieved to see he had not. As she opened the front door and stepped outside, cradling her warm casserole dish in her left arm, she saw a vase of pink tea roses on the ground next to the porch chair. Under the vase was a piece of paper, scribbled with his signature, phone number, and a message: "Vanessa, please call me." Picking up the vase, she carried the flowers inside, impatiently thinking, *Craig, why now?*

Julie's party turned out to be fun and just what Vanessa needed to take her mind off her ex-fiancé's visit. She refused the consultant's offer of a facial, because she already had a favorite line of skin care products. But she ordered enough nail polish, lipstick, and hand lotion to last her a long time. Her purchases also ensured that Julie would reap a nice hostess bonus. The potluck spread was delicious, and she was pleased that all of her macaroni and cheese casserole had been eaten by the other party guests.

Dressed now in her pajamas and sitting on the edge of her bed, Vanessa chatted with her Aunt Rachel whom she had called to discuss Craig's surprise visit. Before calling her aunt, she had tried calling Rita but only got through to her voice mail.

"I always knew he would reach out again, but I didn't know it would take him this long," Aunt Rachel said. "Considering how abrupt your relationship ended, it's time you all meet and talk calmly. You need to see what's on his mind. I don't think you can avoid him."

"Well, that's for sure, especially since he knows my new address and was not shy about dropping by unannounced."

"Vanessa, promise me you'll pray before you speak to him. Ask God to lead and direct you. And if you do that, everything will be all right."

"I promise I'll pray before I call him—and that you're right about everything turning out okay!"

Craig had crossed Vanessa's mind many times since their breakup, but it was only curiosity. She had sometimes wondered what he was currently doing with his life. Her thoughts were never about wanting to rekindle the flame of love that had once shined between them.

Craig was a senior auditor for a top accounting organization when he met Vanessa. After dating for nearly two years, they became engaged. Shortly thereafter, he had unpleasantly surprised her with the news that he had quit his job to pursue a career as a singer. She knew he was passionate about singing—he sang in the church choir and with a local band on weekends—but she never imagined he would consider singing to be anything more than part-time fun. The news of his sudden career change badly strained their relationship. Vanessa believed that unless a person was dealing with enormous job stress or suddenly struck it rich, no one should willingly leave a job until a new one had been confirmed.

When Craig announced that he had quit his job, Vanessa thought of their upcoming nuptials. She wondered if she could trust his judgment on bigger issues, if he could impulsively quit his job without having a sound safety net in place—and without speaking with her about it in advance. She was, after all, his fiancée.

In return, Craig had accused Vanessa of being unsupportive and only interested in his six-figure salary. That assertion had made her laugh out loud. Wasting no time to correct his faulty thinking, she assured him that his income was not a big deal to her, because she was already financially secure. And that was the truth. Her only concern was that he be able to financially support himself, as they made plans together. With Craig the CPA, she imagined a stable future. But with Craig the singer, she imagined a life of highs and lows—mostly lows, because at best she thought he was an average singer. But neither one of them wanted to throw in the towel on their relationship just yet, so they stayed together.

Eventually, however, Vanessa ran out of patience and affection. The two lived separately, but Craig had been spending a lot of time at her place. She grew resentful, watching him sit around, as he waited to hear back from his so-called friends in the entertainment business. They were always promising to hook him up with connections, only they never did. She grew tired of many things—his weekend singing gigs that left no time for them to have fun together—stocking her refrigerator with food only to have him empty it—listening to him defend himself to his parents who, like her, thought he needed to rejoin the corporate work force—and weekly arguments that sprang up out of nowhere. And while he never asked her for money, she knew his savings account was quickly drying up.

A few days before Vanessa's parents' accident, Craig was in Charlotte, North Carolina, visiting friends. He wasn't due back until Sunday night. With time alone to think, Vanessa decided to call off their relationship, at least temporarily. She needed some time apart from him in order to reflect on where they were headed as a couple. After neatly packing up his belongings—the few that were at her apartment—she was eager to see him and send him packing. But since he was not coming back until Sunday night, she decided to drive to Richmond on Saturday morning to visit her parents. They were going to have a relaxing evening, catching up over good food and video movies. Her plan was to spend Saturday night in Richmond and drive back to DC on Sunday to deal with Craig.

But early Saturday morning, Craig had called Vanessa with the news that he was on his way back. He was anxious to see her that evening—and she was anxious to break things off—so she cancelled her plans with her parents. Only he never showed. And he didn't bother to call and give her an update either. Around 5 p.m. that evening, Vanessa called her parents to remind them that she would be home the next weekend. They playfully chided her about canceling on them and told her they were going to visit a friend who had recently gotten out of the hospital.

When Vanessa's phone rang two hours later, she assumed it would be Craig, calling to say that he was back and on his way to her place. Instead, it was the Richmond police calling with news of a fatal collision.

Shocked and grief-stricken, Vanessa told herself that if she had traveled to Richmond as planned, her parents would not have ventured out into the path of destruction. And the only reason she had not gone to Richmond was because of Craig, who said he was coming back that day and did not. Needing to lash out at someone, he was the perfect target. In a fit of anger, she called him with the news of the accident, as well as the news that their relationship was over forever. That was the last time she had talked with him. Now, he was back on the scene.

After saying goodnight to her aunt and hanging up the phone, Vanessa rested her head back on the pillow. With her aunt's request to pray still fresh on her mind—and to honor her own renewed vow to continue strengthening her faith in God—she thought, *Now is as good a time as any to send up a prayer*. Sitting up, she swung her legs over the side of the bed and got down on her knees. It was time to have another talk with God.

Chapter 7

It was 7:50 a.m. Monday morning and Vanessa was racing against time. Standing in her living room, she needed to be four long blocks away at the bus stop in exactly eight minutes to catch the bus for the short ride to the Brookland Metrorail station. If she missed the bus, she would have to wait thirty minutes for the next one—or skip the bus altogether and walk ten blocks to the Metrorail station.

Ordinarily, Vanessa liked walking to the station. Mostly an uphill climb, it was great exercise. She loved her neighborhood, and long walks gave her the opportunity to get to know her neighbors, study landscaping designs, and pick up ideas for home renovation projects. But on this cloudy morning, Vanessa had hit the snooze button on her alarm clock one too many times, and now the rush was on to make a 9 a.m. debrief meeting with the association staff. The convention had officially ended last Friday in New York, but she still had open projects to finalize over the next month.

Placing her pumps into her tote bag, Vanessa quickly slid her stocking feet into her favorite pair of sneakers. After picking up her bag, sweater, and umbrella, she turned on the security alarm system, stepped outside, and locked the door. As she walked off at a brisk pace, suddenly, her cell phone quacked loudly. Smiling, Vanessa knew exactly who was calling, because quacking was an identifying ringtone she had assigned to Rita's phone number.

"Good morning, Rita!"

"Good morning, Sis! I saw on my caller ID that you called over the week-end, but I haven't had a good chunk of time to myself until now to call you back. I figured since you didn't leave a message, it wasn't urgent. So how're you doing? I know you're glad to be back in DC."

"Yes, I am! And I'm okay, but I'm rushing to catch a bus."

"Well, I don't want to get between you and that bus, but I have to know what you think about Elliott. I was expecting to hear from you Friday night after *your date*."

"I know I should have called, but it was late when I got back to the hotel and I was just too exhausted to talk." Vanessa passed on teasing Rita about Mike's text message to Elliott.

Rita chuckled. "Since when have you ever been too tired to talk?"

Vanessa smiled. "How come you didn't mention that Elliott was a widower with a young daughter?"

Rita said, "Girl, you put up such a fuss about meeting the man that I decided to shut my mouth and let him tell you."

Vanessa chuckled.

"I know it's only been a couple of days, but have you heard from him?"

"No, I haven't. But I'd really like to!"

"According to Mike, Elliott said he enjoyed meeting you."

"Enjoyed meeting me?" *Well, that's nice and polite, but not the exciting feedback I was hoping to hear,* she thought.

Since her evening with Elliott, Vanessa had browsed the Internet, fishing for more particulars about him. She had uncovered a wealth of positive information. His biographical sketch on the law firm's website confirmed what he had told her about graduating from Brown University and earning his law degree from Harvard University. A Google search was more revealing, as it showed his past and present board memberships with several notable nonprofit organizations in the DC metropolitan area. He was a civil rights advocate and contributed a generous amount of his time and money to important social causes. And there were photos of him in the midst of DC's society crowds, looking handsome, confident, and worthy to be there. Vanessa had noted there were as many women as men at the events Elliott attended—they were probably all throwing themselves at him! After logging off the computer, she had felt a little out of his league, like she might not be fascinating enough to hold his attention.

On the phone, Rita was saying, "Trust me, he's going to call you. Of course, you can always call him."

"I could, but I prefer the man to take the initiative in the beginning. I'm just old-fashioned that way. Blame it on my dad who always said I should play it cool and let a man pursue me."

"Okay, I hear you. But don't play it too cool. This is a new day, Sister!"

Vanessa laughed. "Speaking of pursuing, I had a surprise visitor yesterday."

"Who?"

"Craig."

"Craig!" Rita shrieked. "What does he want? And where's he been all this time?"

Now reaching the end of the third block, Vanessa looked ahead to see if the bus was in sight. Seeing it at a distance, she picked up her pace. "I don't know, Rita."

"What do you mean you don't know? Weren't you there?"

"He left a vase of pink tea roses and a note on my front porch." Vanessa didn't share that she was at home but hesitant to open the door, because that would lead Rita to ask another round of questions that she didn't have time for this morning.

Rita grunted. "Roses? What's up with that? I hope he's not trying to ease his way back into your life."

"I hope not either—he'll be disappointed," Vanessa said, joining a few others at the bus stop. "Whatever he wants, I'll find out in due time. I'll probably call him today."

"Well, after you talk with him, call me! I'm curious to know what he's up to."

"You know what they say about curiosity, don't you?"

Rita laughed. "You know I would have been gone a long time ago if that were true!"

"That makes two of us!" Vanessa smiled. "I've really got to hang up and catch my bus. I'll talk with you later, okay?"

"Okay, love you!"

"Love you back!" And with that, she shut down her cell phone and stepped back from the curb, as the bus roared to a stop in front of her.

Thirty minutes later, Vanessa exited the gate at the downtown Metrorail station. When she reached the escalator tunnel, she saw a long line of frustrated-looking people. *Oh, no,* she sighed, taking in the sight of the broken escalator. She looked over at the elevator in the far corner of the station, and that line was even longer. *Feet don't fail me now*, she thought, as she merged her way into the line and started climbing the steep steps to the ground level.

Walking up the escalator, Vanessa heard a strong male voice singing what had been her father's favorite Christian song, "How Great Thou Art." The voice was coming from the street level, floating down into the station, and the song brightened her spirit. As she reached the ground level, Vanessa scanned the crowd to find the man behind the voice. He was standing to the side of the station entry, head raised high to the sky, singing the final verse. She had no time to spare, but she stopped anyway. When the man finished singing, Vanessa reached in the pocket of her tote bag, pulled out several dollar bills and dropped them in the baseball cap the man had placed on the ground for contributions.

"Thank you," he whispered.

Vanessa protested. "No, thank you." Looking into his eyes, she said, "Every day I need to spiritually feed my soul and declare how great God is! You helped me with that today."

Others took her lead and placed money in the singer's cap. As Vanessa walked away, the man called out, "God bless you!"

Chapter 8

Vanessa closed her office door and plopped down in her chair, a big smile on her face. The debrief meeting had ended minutes earlier, and it had gone well. As she guided the staff through various convention categories, she had taken careful notes on their comments—in particular on what they felt went well—and had asked for their ideas for next year. She reported that a survey was going out tomorrow by email to all attendees, including sponsors, speakers, and exhibitors. She expected the analysis to be completed within two weeks and would schedule a final and deeper debrief session to review it and identify action steps for next year's convention.

As she pulled out her day planner to look at her calendar, she noticed at the top of today's action list was the note she entered last night: "Call Craig." Since yesterday, she had imagined different ways the conversation could go. But in the end, she had no idea what she would or would not say to him until they were on the phone together. *Come on*, she told herself, *stop procrastinating and call him!*

She started to punch in Craig's number but hung up quickly when she remembered her aunt's request that she pray first. Taking a deep breath, she prayed inwardly, *Dear God, please keep my spirit calm as I talk with Craig. I pray that my words will heal and not hurt. I thank you in advance for blessing this conversation.* Then she placed her call.

The phone rang three times before a male voice said, "Hello?"

Her voice reflected no emotion as she said, "Hi, Craig, it's me, Vanessa."

"Vanessa!" Craig said cheerfully. "I didn't think you'd call, but I'm glad you did. So, how've you been?"

Vanessa didn't know what to say. *How have I been since when exactly—eighteen months ago or do you mean this morning?* She didn't like how-have-you-been questions since she thought most people who ask them are not deeply interested in the answer. She decided to give Craig the answer he would most likely be comfortable hearing. "I'm fine," she said.

"That's great! I'm glad to hear it."

"And you?" She truly was interested in the answer.

"For the most part, I'm all right. I guess I shouldn't complain about anything since it won't help anyway, will it?" Vanessa could hear a smile in Craig's voice.

"Probably not," she agreed.

"You know, I should apologize for stopping by your home yesterday without calling you first, but I assure you it was spontaneous. Yesterday was our special day and I wanted to see you."

Vanessa was confused. *Our special day?*

"Correction!" he said quickly. "It was *supposed to be* our special day."

Vanessa was silent as she now realized what he was talking about.

"You must still be angry with me if you don't remember the date we were supposed to get married," he said with a loud sigh.

Vanessa thought back in time to the day Craig had proposed to her. It was a spring day and the weather couldn't make up its mind whether to rain or shine, so it did both at once. Walking around the Tidal Basin to see the cherry blossom trees, he had wrapped his arms around her and proposed. They were so happy in each other's arms they didn't even notice it had started to rain. Caught without umbrellas, they were drenched in the downpour, and Vanessa had caught a cold that left her feeling miserable all the following week.

"No," she said calmly. "It's not that I'm still angry. I've just been extremely preoccupied with work."

"Well, I'm glad you're not mad at me anymore. So, can we get together and talk?"

"I'm not sure that's a good idea, Craig," Vanessa said, trying to keep her voice level. "I don't see the point in getting together and rehashing old stuff that's best left in the past. We've been through enough—at least I know I certainly have."

Craig shook his head in defeat. He didn't want to press Vanessa if she didn't want to see him. But when he opened his mouth to say that he understood her decision, his true emotions tumbled out. "Please, Vanessa, I *really* need to see you!"

Vanessa looked to the sky. *Lord, order my steps,* she prayed. Then, looking down at her calendar, she heard herself saying, "Okay, fine — let's meet. I'm free on Saturday. Is noon okay?"

"Yeah, noontime is perfect!" he confirmed hurriedly, locking her into the commitment. "Should I come to your house?"

"No, let's meet somewhere else," she said quickly. "I'll think of a place and let you know by Friday."

"Vanessa, I can't wait to see you."

Since that was a sentiment she didn't share, she said, "Well, I guess I'll talk with you later." And with that, their first conversation since that dreadful night eighteen months ago was over.

Vanessa pushed back her chair and walked over to the window. All the upbeat energy she had felt before talking with Craig was now falling hard like the rain outside the window. With the debrief meeting over and no pressing matters on her afternoon schedule, the only thing she wanted to do on this rainy day was go back home, crawl into bed, drape herself in her mother's soft handmade quilt and sleep away the day.

And so she did.

After a long afternoon nap, Vanessa woke to the sound of rain, pounding against her bedroom window. Lightly tossing back her quilt, she sat upright in the bed. As she listened to the rain, she remembered back to her childhood and how one day when she had complained about a rainy day her father told her, "Behind all the falling rain, the sun still hangs in the sky. And if the sun can hang in there through the rain, surely you can, too." Vanessa sighed. *Great advice, Daddy,* she thought. *I'm hanging in here!*

Looking for a distraction, Vanessa picked up her cell phone that was in muted mode on the table beside the bed. There were a dozen new messages in her work email account. After quickly scanning each one, she decided that a reply on each of them could wait until tomorrow.

Turning on the television, she watched the 4 p.m. news. But instead of listening to the anchors break down the news events, she leaned back on her pillows and closed her eyes, allowing her mind to pleasantly drift back to just a few days ago when she met Elliott. She wondered what he was doing at this moment and if he might possibly be thinking about her.

Why do I bother with questions about things I may never know the answer to? Vanessa thought.

Chapter 9

Over the next few days, Vanessa's focal point shifted from matters of the heart, back to event planning. With projects to wrap up and new ones to take on, she had a lot on her plate.

Arriving home late from the office on Thursday evening, Vanessa was hungry. She had only eaten an apple and a handful of grapes for lunch. As she opened her refrigerator, she frowned. *When was the last time I bought groceries?* Picking up the milk carton and shaking it, she wondered if there was enough for a bowl of cereal. *Wait, do I have any?* Turning, she opened the cabinet and saw an unopened box of an organic brand of cereal complete with nuts and berries. *It'll have to do because I'm not going back out tonight.*

After finishing a bowl of cereal, Vanessa took a shower, slipped on her pajamas, and climbed into bed. Nestled down comfortably under the sheets and quilt, she turned on the television and flipped through several cable channels in search of *Law and Order* reruns. There were none to be found. Just as she got interested in a movie on the LMN Network, she heard a burst of melody coming from her cell phone on the table by the bed. She picked it up and read the incoming text message: "Do you like blueberry pancakes? If so, call me. If not, please call anyway. Elliott Reeves."

A wide smile stretched across Vanessa's face. *Well, well, well—I was beginning to think you had lost my number!* Picking up the phone to call him, she stopped herself just before punching the last two numbers. Her smiled waned as she thought, *Elliott took six days to reach out to me, so maybe I shouldn't be so quick on the dial.* She disconnected from the call and placed the phone back on the table. But minutes later, she thought, *Get real—this is no time to play games!* She picked up phone and dialed his number.

Elliott answered on the second ring. "Vanessa, hello! I'm glad you called me!"

"Well, how could I not after reading your text about blueberry pancakes. I like them very much!"

Elliott laughed. "I'm glad to hear it because my daughter tells me that I make the best blueberry pancakes in the world. Of course, I don't let that go to my head because she hasn't traveled very much." Pausing long enough to hear Vanessa chuckle, Elliott continued, "Anyway, on weekend mornings, I make them for her along with whatever else she wants to eat."

Lucky little girl, Vanessa thought. "Elliott, you're really making me hungry." Her stomach growled, agreeing with her.

"Well, that's good because I'm wondering if you're available to join me and Nicole for breakfast on Saturday."

Vanessa smiled. *This is a unique invitation,* she thought. *Not lunch or dinner but breakfast.* "Yeah, I think I can make it," she said cheerfully. "What time are you serving these best-in-the-world pancakes?"

"I'm flexible on the time, but we usually have breakfast around 9 a.m."

"That works for me. Can I bring anything—pastries or fresh fruit?"

"No, just bring a big appetite. I'm looking forward to seeing you again."

Vanessa smiled. "Thanks! It'll be good seeing you, too."

"So, how've you been feeling this week?"

"Compared to last week's emotional drain, I feel much stronger now that I'm back at home."

"I'm glad to hear it. I've thought about you, praying you were feeling better."

Vanessa smiled. "Thanks, I appreciate it."

"Oh, before I forget, I'm taking Nicole to the American History Museum after breakfast. She has a school project on one of the exhibits. You're welcome to join us, if you like."

Remembering her plans at noon with Craig, Vanessa frowned. "I love museums, but I'll have to take a pass this time. I've got a date with my past."

"A date with your past, huh?"

Why did I say that? she thought. But now that it was hanging out there, she exhaled softly and continued. "My ex-fiancé called this week and wants to talk, so we're meeting Saturday afternoon."

An ex-fiancé, Elliott thought with a touch of gloom. "How long ago did you all break up?"

"I called off our relationship a year and a half ago."

"Why? What happened?" Quickly regretting the questions, Elliott said, "Wait, I apologize for asking. You don't have to answer!"

Vanessa paused. "No, it's fine to ask," she said. "To make a long story short, we fell out of sync with our dreams as a couple—we wanted different things." She explained to him how the end of her relationship with Craig played into the timeline of her parents' accident. With a sigh, Vanessa said, "And whenever I think back on it, the whole thing just makes me angry all over again."

Elliott asked softly, "Why's that, Vanessa?"

"Craig interfered with my plans. I believe that if I'd gone to Richmond, my parents would be alive today. We would have all been together at home that Saturday evening." She paused a moment and then said, "But of course, I'm not blameless—I could have gone to see my parents anyway and just waited to talk with him another day. I don't know. I go back and forth—first blaming Craig and then myself."

Elliott was silent for several moments. Finally he spoke. "I'm thinking about what you said about not going to Richmond because of Craig's phone call. But, if I flip that around, I could argue that his call might have actually saved your life. You could have been in that accident with your parents."

Elliott's words halted Vanessa. In all this time, she had never considered that she *could have been* in the accident. She had only considered the scenario of the three of them safe and sound at home together. Now, reflecting on the alternative, she said slowly, as if thinking out loud. "I hear what you're saying, but I had talked with my parents and we'd made plans to stay home...so I don't think we'd have changed our minds and gone out..."

"I understand this is difficult," Elliott injected tenderly. "The only point I'm trying to make is that you don't know with absolute certainty what would have happened had you gone to Richmond. You all could have stayed home, and then again you could have easily changed your minds and gone out to visit friends or whatever. Things can change on a dime, Vanessa, and blaming yourself for the accident is a terrible weight to carry around, or to put on somebody else. The only person at fault was the driver of the other car; it's just that plain and simple."

And yet sadly enough, I struggle with what's plain and simple. But I don't want to keep struggling with it, Vanessa thought. Sighing appreciatively at his words, she said, "Elliott, thank you. You're a great listener. And I appreciate your calm and rationale reasoning on things. You must win a lot of your court cases."

With a smile, Elliott said, "I do all right." The truth is that Elliott did better than all right. He was a top litigator, a much sought after attorney with a winning reputation. "But what's important is that you know you're not to blame for anything."

Vanessa took a deep breath and replied, "I really want to believe that!" Pausing, she said with a smile in her voice, "I think I need to stop sounding so emotionally fragile, or you'll take back your breakfast invitation."

Elliott chuckled lightly and said, "No way, my lady. We've got a breakfast date! I think you're amazing, and I'm glad to know you."

"Thanks, and I'm equally glad to know you."

In an effort to make her laugh, he asked, "So what...I'm not equally amazing?"

Vanessa laughed. "Hmmm, I'd like to taste those blueberry pancakes of yours before I use the word *amazing*."

Elliott tossed back his head and laughed. "Okay, fair enough! You know, after a big breakfast, you might not have much appetite for lunch." Teasing her, he asked, "Are you sure you need to keep your afternoon plans?"

Vanessa replied slowly, "Yeah...I do...especially since things didn't end amicably. Maybe now is our chance to make that happen."

"I really hope so," Elliott said. "Well, Vanessa, it's getting late so I'm going to let you hang up and get some sleep. I'll see you on Saturday morning. You have my address, but call if you need directions."

"I will, and thanks again for the invite."

Vanessa was still on Elliott's mind an hour after their conversation had ended. He had wanted to call her earlier in the week, but had waited, giving himself time to think clearly about his next move with her.

Since Lisa's death, Elliott had gone out with several interesting women but never invited them to his home or to meet Nicole. He had purposely kept light friendships with them. His heart wasn't ready for anything intense, and he wanted to fully focus on Nicole's needs without the distraction of a new romance competing for his attention. But now, with enough time gone by, he felt ready to embrace a serious relationship—but only with someone extra special; a woman with a heart big enough to embrace both him and Nicole. From what he had personally observed of Vanessa and researched on his own, his instincts told him that she just might be that special woman. He was anxious to find out.

Chapter 10

Vanessa's alarm clock went off at 7 a.m. on Saturday morning. Turning off the alarm, she laid back and stretched her limbs fully to get her mind and body ready to take on the day. Climbing out of bed, she headed for the shower wondering what to wear today to meet not one, but two men: one from her past and—hopefully—the other for her future. Smiling at the thought of her future, she said out loud, "A woman can dream!"

Forty minutes later, Vanessa was comfortably dressed in a new pair of black jeans and a black-and-white, three-quarter sleeve tunic blouse. She had minimized her makeup—applying only a sunscreen moisturizer, a touch of liner in the corner of her eyes, and a natural shade of lip gloss. She was going for the casual look since Elliott has already seen her more fashionable side. After brushing and styling her hair, she put on her favorite pair of gold hoop earrings before adding the final touch—a new pair of black sandals that highlighted her fresh pedicure.

As Vanessa drove to Elliott's home in DC's Crestwood neighborhood, the excitement of seeing him again was building. She had sent him a text message to let him know that she was on her way. *God, please bless this new friendship*, she thought as she turned the car on to his street and looked for his address.

From his living room window, Elliott saw Vanessa drive up in her Volkswagen Beetle and park in his driveway. As she exited her car, he went to the front door, opening it wide for a warm welcome. Stepping outside on his front porch, he smiled brightly as she walked toward him carrying a big bouquet of yellow daisies.

As Vanessa walked up the steps of Elliott's home, she was grateful he couldn't hear her thumping heart, beating with excitement. Dressed casually, he was wearing a pair of black athletic pants, a white jersey top, and a pair of white sneakers. *He looks more like a handsome star athlete today than a lawyer,* she thought.

"Vanessa, I'm happy to see you!" Elliott said, reaching out his hand to help her up the last two steps.

Vanessa smiled, placing her hand into his. "Thanks for inviting me!"

"Come inside," he said, opening the door. The delicious aromas of coffee and cuisine enveloped his home, immediately relaxing Vanessa's spirit.

"You told me not to bring anything, but I couldn't resist bringing flowers for the table."

Elliott happily accepted the bouquet. "Nicole loves daisies—thanks for bringing them!"

Glancing around, Vanessa smiled. "Your home is lovely, and it smells delicious!"

Elliott chuckled. "It's probably the hazelnut coffee." Extending his hand toward the living room, he said, "Please look around and get comfortable while I find a vase." Heading for the kitchen, Elliott passed a mahogany staircase and called up, "Baby girl, come down and meet my friend, Vanessa."

While she waited, Vanessa admired the attractively decorated living room. It was stylish and contemporary with comfortable furniture, gleaming hardwood floors, a white marble fireplace, and colorful art on the wall. *This room looks like a beautiful picture in a magazine,* she thought.

At the sound of footsteps on the staircase, Vanessa turned and looked directly into the round, expressive eyes of the pretty girl she had seen in a photo a week ago.

"Hi, I'm Nicole," the girl said with a smile that showed off her marble-size dimples. Her hair was brushed into a ponytail and clamped with a pink barrette. Dressed in blue jeans topped with a pink and green peasant-style shirt, she looked adorable.

"Hi, I'm Vanessa. I'm happy to meet you," she said, reaching forward and softly shaking the hand that Nicole extended to her.

"Thanks. I'm glad you could come. You're going to love my dad's pancakes."

Before Vanessa could respond, Elliott called out from the dining room, "Okay, ladies, breakfast is ready."

Nicole looked at Vanessa and whispered, "Breakfast is a big deal in our house, especially on the weekends."

Vanessa smiled and whispered back to her, "Yes, I see it is!"

Walking into the dining room, Vanessa marveled at the cheerfully decorated table filled with platters of scrambled eggs, turkey bacon, grits, and, of course, blueberry pancakes. The daisies she had brought were in a vase and now serving as their centerpiece.

Joining hands to say grace, Elliott asked Nicole to bless the food and she did, offering up a sweet, child-size prayer. For the first few minutes, no one spoke as they settled in to eat, drizzling syrup on their pancakes. When Vanessa took her first bite, she closed her eyes to savor its amazingly wonderful blueberry taste and unwittingly let out a murmur of contentment. Realizing that she had moaned out loud, she opened her eyes to find Elliott and Nicole watching her with enjoyment. "What's wrong with you two?" she playfully demanded. "Haven't you ever seen a woman *really enjoy* her food before?"

Nicole giggled. "Nope, not like that."

Amused, Elliott said, "My first time, too—I think I really like it!"

Vanessa smiled and said, "Well, pass the bacon and sit back. You all are in for a treat."

Nicole looked at Vanessa and grinned. Already, she was enjoying her dad's new friend.

After a delicious breakfast mixed with lively conversation and laughter, they gathered in the family room to play one of Nicole's Wii video games. With her eyes glued to the Super Mario game with its animated explosions and sparks, Nicole completely missed the sparks of chemistry flowing between her dad and Vanessa.

Elliott and Vanessa sat across from each other with game remotes in hand, reflecting less on the moves of Super Mario and more on what friendly move to make next on each other. But Elliott knew he had to move cautiously now that Vanessa had reunion plans in an hour with a man she had once loved enough to almost marry.

Chapter 11

S itting on a bench built for two, in one of the flower gardens of a monastery in DC's Brookland neighborhood, Craig looked at his watch. It was a few minutes before noon. Surrounded by trees, flowers, birds, and squirrels, he thought, *Only Vanessa would come up with the idea to meet in this kind of setting. I hope she shows up.*

Meanwhile, Vanessa sat in her parked car in the monastery's parking lot, willing herself to get her meeting with Craig over. But her thoughts of Elliott and Nicole and the enjoyable morning they had shared together kept her immobilized. Looking at her watch, she imagined they were now at the American History Museum and wished she was with them. Summoning up the will to move, Vanessa exited her car and walked quickly across the street. She was glad she had thought of the garden grounds as today's meeting place. Some months ago she had toured the grounds as a possible site for a client's social event. Afterward, she'd returned for her own benefit, because it was an ideal place to reflect and meditate. Since today was all about healing the past, she wanted a peaceful setting to influence the outcome.

The grounds were full of visitors today, and there were several nuns standing near Craig, admiring a bush of red roses. He noticed that one elderly nun kept glancing at him with a little smile on her face. He chuckled inwardly as he remembered a movie he had watched a few days ago on the classics station. Sidney Poitier had starred in it. The movie was *Lilies of the Field,* and it was about a traveling handyman who helped build a chapel for a group of nuns. *I hope she doesn't think I've been sent from God to build her a chapel,* he thought, amused. At that moment, a fearless squirrel in search of a nut scampered along the path and stopped and looked at him.

Craig pulled out his cell phone and glanced at it. Nothing from Vanessa. As he slipped it back into his pocket, he looked up to see that she was standing a few feet away, staring at him thoughtfully. An emotional wave washed over him. Shaking it off, he stood to greet her as she walked toward him.

"Vanessa," he said softly. *How did I mess things up so badly with this pretty woman?*

"Hi, Craig," Vanessa said, giving him a hesitant smile. "Did you have any trouble finding this place?"

Smiling brightly, he said, "No problem at all. I'll always find my way to you."

Vanessa thought, *Yeah, and it only took you a year and a half!* Not sure whether to hug him or not, she leaned in for a light embrace. And when she did, Craig wrapped her in his arms and pulled her close. Surprised by the intensity of the hug, she accepted his embrace for a brief moment before gently pulling away.

"Let's sit down," she said. Craig was a nice-looking man with dark, chiseled features. He was about ten pounds heavier than when she last saw him, but he was carrying it well given his height. She noticed that he hadn't shaved in a few days and wondered if he was trying to grow a beard. He had had one when they first met. His eyes looked puffy and watery. *Most likely allergies*, she thought. He suffered from them year round.

When they sat down, Craig said, "I'm glad you agreed to meet me."

Remembering how close she had come last night to cancelling, Vanessa replied, "Yeah, well, I almost changed my mind."

Surprised, he eyed her silently before asking, "Why? Are you afraid of something?"

"No, not at all," she said quickly. "What would I possibly be afraid of?"

Looking Vanessa firmly in her eyes, Craig said, "Finding out that you're still in love with me, as I am with you."

Vanessa studied his serious expression, and a wave of annoyance washed over her. Remembering Aunt Rachel's advice to pray before speaking, she only had time to think, *Lord, help me!*

"Craig, I don't know how you feel, but I want you to know that's not true for me."

Momentarily deflated, he shifted his eyes downward.

A Saint
Saved by
Grace

By Pastor James Graham

"You can find this life-changing book on Amazon.com"

Pastor James Graham can be reached at:
Christian Corner Fellowship
P.O. Box 653
Napanoch, New York 12458
www.facebook.com/christiancornerfellowshipinc

Published: June 2014
Publisher: Create Space
ISBN -13:9781500312978 # located on back cover of this publication
The King James Version of The Bible is used in this publication. Some passages have been slightly modified for clarity of some Old English style words and language.

This Publication is dedication to my Wonderful
Wife, Kirsten and my two lovely daughters.
I thank God for the ministry that
He has entrusted our family with.

*"God Bless you Christian Corner Fellowship Family!
God has truly blessed us. In the Name of Jesus, we
will walk in victory as Saints saved by Grace!"*

Table of Contents

Introduction

For all have sinned, and come short of the glory of God.
But now we Christians are justified freely by His Grace,
through the redemption that is in Christ Jesus found in
Romans 3:23-24. Many in the "church world" would be
shocked to learn that one cannot be Saved by Grace and a
Sinner at the same time. Either you're Saved by Grace or
you're a Sinner.

The Bible states: "But God commended his love toward us,
in that, while we were yet sinners, Christ died for us."-
Romans 5:8. All one has to do is receive God's Grace,
which is the forgiveness of sin by Christ, who was
predestined to die for the sins of the world.

Receiving Grace means that all though you have sinned
and come short of the glory of God, you have repented,
and received God's Grace. That Grace is given through His
Only Begotten Son Jesus Christ.

While Sinners on the other hand have sinned and come
short of the glory of God, and have not repented, at the
same time rejecting God's Grace. Being a "Sinner Saved by
Grace" is an oxymoron….it is a contradiction. You're either
Saved by Grace or you're a Sinner. It's time for the church
to stand up and make its claim "I'm a Saint Saved by
Grace!"

*"For by grace you have been saved through faith, and that
not of yourselves: it is the gift of God."- Ephesians 2:8*

Section 1

<u>There is something you can do to receive God's Grace!</u>

First, the bible commands all of mankind to repent from their sins. You have to do something: repent. This is an act of will. This act is done by individual choice, your free will. You must do something to repent, and that is turn from your wicked ways.

Secondly, by receiving God's Grace, you have to do something. You have to accept His Grace. How do you accept God's Grace? You confess Jesus as Lord and Savior and believed in your heart that God raised him from the dead. No, you did nothing to generate God's Grace; it is His Gift to you.

But it is something you have to do...receive it. The choice is yours, receive or reject God's Grace. It is a mindset, a heart condition, a willingness to place your faith in the hands of God through His Son Jesus Christ.

The following scriptures support section 1 subtitle:
"There is something you can do to receive God's Grace!"

From that time Jesus began to preach, and to say, Repent:
for the kingdom of heaven is at hand.
-Matthew 4:17

Then Peter said unto them, Repent, and be baptized every
one of you in the name of Jesus Christ for the remission of
sin, and ye shall receive the gift of the Holy Ghost.
-Acts 2:38

And the times of this ignorance God winked at: but now
commanded all men everywhere to repent: Because He
hath appointed a day, in the which he will judge the world
in righteousness by that Man whom He hath ordained;
whereof He hath given assurance unto all men, in that He
hath raised him from the dead.
-Acts 17:30-31

That if you shalt confess with thy mouth the Lord Jesus,
and shalt believe in thine heart that God hath raised him
from the dead, thou shalt be saved.
-Romans 10:9

Section 2

Repentance: Key to those in Sin, yet not Sinners.

Many in the "church world" would be surprised to learn that one can sin and still not be a sinner, as long as they repent and receive God's Grace. In God's eyes, sin is not imputed to those who repent, or unknowingly sin. God is always looking to forgive; He is most gracious in this regard. On the other hand, a Sinner is defined by biblical standards and examples, as one who does not repent, and or knowingly sin; defending, excusing, and covering up their wicked ways. Sinners reject God's Grace.

Case and Point: The First siblings of humanity, Cain and Abel, sons of Adam and Eve were both born into sin. Chances are both sinned. But Cain became a sinner, while Abel became Righteous. Why? Cain's motives were knowingly selfish (sinful), putting self before God. While Abel's motives were selfless putting God before self.

 God's Grace would warn Cain about his motives and actions, and the consequence if he did not repent.
 God said to Cain "If thou doest well, shalt thou not be accepted? If thou do not well, sin lies at the door. And unto thee shall be his desire…"- Genesis 3:7. God was giving Cain a chance to repent "If thou doest well, shalt thou not be accepted?" in other words "do the right thing!" Repenting is turning from the wrong path, to the right path.

Cain would reject God's Grace, and the consequence of Cain's actions coupled with his selfish motives and actions would result in "The Spirit of Sin" ruling over him. Sin stands at the door of everyone who rejects God's Grace, while embracing a lifestyle of selfish motives and actions. Sin desires to rule over all who does not receive God's Grace, and in return those persons become its servants and slaves.

Meanwhile, we see Abel. Even though Abel was born in an atmosphere of sin, he knew what was right and God received and respected him. In God's eyes, as long as Abel remained in this lifestyle, sin would not be imputed to Abel, even though sin was present in his life. God is always looking to forgive; He is most gracious in this regard.

In Summary, Both Cain and Abel was born in Sin and shaped in iniquity. Both came short of the glory of God. Yet one was a Sinner and one was a Saint, because of the choices they made concerning their relationship to God. One received and one rejected his Grace. We are to come to God like Abel (Hebrew 11:4) and not Cain (1 John 3:12).

The following Scriptures will support the subtitle:
"Repentance: Key to those who Sin, yet not Sinners."

Behold, I was shaped in iniquity: and in sin did my mother conceive me. Behold, thou desires truth in the inward parts: and in the hidden part thou shalt make me to know wisdom.
-Psalm 51:5-6

Jesus said unto them, if ye were blind, ye should have no sin: but now ye say, we see; therefore your sin remains.
-John 9:41

If I had not come and spoken unto them, they had not had sin: but now they have no cover for their sin.
-John 15:22

Blessed is the man to whom The LORD will not impute sin.
-Romans 4:8
(*taken from Psalm 32:2)

For until the law sin was in the world: but sin is not imputed when there is no law.
-Romans 5:13

If we say that we have not sinned, we make him a liar, and his word is not in us.
-1 John 1:10

Whosoever abides in him sin not: whosoever sin hath not seen him, neither known him.
-1 John 3:6

Other Voices out there saying: I'm a Saint, not a Sinner.

"Followers of Christ should never identify themselves as sinners, as in the present tense. Yes, we were once sinners, But after we accept Christ and repent of our sins we are no longer sinners. Either I am saved and therefore a saint, or I am lost and therefore, a sinner. I cannot be both."

-April Banks
Examiner.com
June 15, 2011

"Just a sinner saved by grace" is only half the gospel. It's true in Christ, God has wiped the slate clean and has forgiven us our sins, but He also regenerates us through the power of His Spirit. God is restoring our relationship to Him. He is living within us."

-Trevin Wax
Thegospelcoalition.org
June 11, 2012

You're a Saint-Not a "Sinner Saved by grace." You may need to read that heading again, you're a saint, a holy one. Not understanding this causes us to view ourselves differently than God does.

-Andrew Jenkins
Andrejenkins.wordpress.com
March 20, 2013

Section 3

God's Grace calls Sinners to Repentance

The first time the word "Grace" is used in the Bible was towards Noah, in the land of Eden, when God was readying heaven to destroy the earth because of its wickedness (Genesis 6:8). The Bible states that Noah was a preacher of righteous, meaning he was preaching repentance and the coming of Our Lord (2 Peter 2:5).

Before this time, God's Grace would translate a man called Enoch of the 7th Generation of humanity, foreseeing the trend of Mankind's wickedness. God's Grace would also give Enoch revelation of Christ in the land of Eden, Jude 14 states Enoch prophesied of these, saying, Behold, the Lord cometh with ten thousands of his saints. Yes even Humanity in the land of Eden was looking for Christ.

God's Grace would also reveal to Adam and Eve that Christ would come from "the seed of the woman" foreshowing how Christ would be born, of a virgin by The Holy Ghost (Genesis 3:15 and Luke 1:31-33). Looking back at Noah, when all looked lost, Noah found Grace with God, and received revelation on how to escape the destruction to come. And all the while, God's Grace was working with Mankind giving them hope and calling Sinners to Repentance.

The following scriptures support the subtitle:
"God's Grace calls Sinners to Repentance."

But go ye and learn what that meant, I will have mercy, and not sacrifice: for I am not come to call the righteous, but sinners to repentance.
-Matthew 9:13

I say unto you, that likewise joy shall be in heaven over one sinner that repented, more than over ninety and nine just person, which need no repentance.
-Luke 15:7
(**Even though both the sinner and the Just sins, the just repents, while the sinner does not.)

Let him know, that he which converts the sinner from the error of his way shall save a soul from death, and shall hide a multitude of sins.
-James 5:20
(**Saints can convert sinners with the Gospel of Jesus Christ.)

Section 4

The Saints

The Saints in the New Testament are fellow heirs with the Saints in the Old Testament (Ephesians 2:19). Both have one important thing in common, that is, Christ. The Saints of the Old Testament was looking for Christ to come, while the New Testament Saints saw Christ.

Saints who came after those who saw Christ are told of his words, works and ways, while the Holy Ghost within us verifies that these accounts are true (John 15:16-17). Saints are not without sin, but they do repent of sin, and receive God's Grace in His Son Jesus Christ (1 John 1:9).

The following Scriptures are about The Saints:

Likewise, the Spirit also helps our infirmities: for we know not what we should pray for as we ought: but the Spirit itself makes intercession for us with groaning which cannot be uttered. And he that searches the heart knows what is the mind of the Spirit, because he makes intercession for **the saints** according to the will of God.
-Romans 9:26-27

The Blessings of the Saint

The eyes of your understanding being enlightened: that ye may know what is the hope of his calling, and what the riches of glory of his inheritance in **the saints**. And what is the exceeding greatness of his power to us-ward who believes, according to the working of his mighty power.
-Ephesians 1:18-19

The Chastisement of the Saint

For whom the LORD loves he chastens, and scourge every son who he receives.
-Hebrews 12:6 (Proverbs 3:11)

Section 5

The Sinners

The Sinners are those who make excuses for sin, defend sin, and embrace sin. They do not repent of sins and reject God's Grace.

The Following scriptures are about the sinners:

Knowing this, that the law is not made for a righteous man, but for the lawless and disobedient, for the ungodly and for **sinners**, for unholy and profane, for murderers of fathers and murderers of mothers, for manslayers, for whoremongers, for them that defile themselves with mankind, for men stealers, for liars, for perjured persons, and if there be any other thing that is contrary to sound doctrine; to the glorious gospel of the blessed God, this was committed to my trust.
-1 Timothy 1:9-11

Submit yourselves therefore to God. Resist the devil, and he will flee from you. Draw nigh to God, and he will draw nigh to you. Cleanse your hands, ye **sinners**; and purify your hearts, ye double minded.
-James 4:7-8

To execute judgment upon all, and to convince all that are ungodly among them of all their ungodly deeds which they have ungodly deeds which they have ungodly committed, and of all their hard speeches which **ungodly sinners** have spoken against him. These are murmurers, complainers, walking after their own lusts: and their mouth speaks great swelling words, having men's persons in admiration because of advantage.
-Jude15-16

Consequences for Sin and Sinners
And if your right hand causes you to sin, cut if off and cast it from you for it is more profitable for you that one of your members perish, than for your whole body to be cast into hell.
-Matthew 5:30

And do not fear those who kill the body but cannot kill the soul. But rather fear Him who is able to destroy both soul and body in hell.
-Matthew 10:28

And being in torments in Hell, he lifted up his eyes and saw Abraham afar off, and Lazarus in his bosom. The he cried and said, "Father Abraham, have mercy on me, and send Lazarus that he may dip the tip of his finger in water and cool my tongue; for I am tormented in this flame."
-Luke 16:23-24

...why hast thou conceived this thing in thine heart? Thou hast not lied unto men, but unto God. And Ananias hearing these words fell down, and gave up the ghost: and great fear came on all them that heard these things.
-Acts 5:4-5 (Matthew 12:31)

Section 6

The Apostle Paul was a Saint, and not a Sinner.

In church we hear too often that Apostle Paul viewed himself as a "Sinner saved by grace"....this could be farthest from the truth. All throughout the New Testament, we read and learn that the Apostle Paul viewed himself as one who was a sinner in the past, was saved by Grace in the present and through Jesus Christ, became a Saint. The Apostle Paul was a Saint saved by Grace. The Apostle Paul was also keenly aware of his calling: to preach and teach the Gentiles about Christ according to Romans 15:26.

The Following scriptures support the subtitle:
"The Apostle Paul was a Saint, and not a Sinner."

For if the truth of God hath more abounded through my lie unto his glory; why yet am I also judged as **a sinner?**
-Romans 3:7
(**The Apostle Paul did not view himself as a sinner.)

Unto me, who am less than the least of **all saints**, is this grace given, that I should preach among the Gentiles the unsearchable riches of Christ...
-Ephesians 3:8
(**The Apostle Paul viewed himself as
a saint and not a sinner.)

This is a faithful saying and worthy of all acceptation, that Christ Jesus came into the world to **save sinners**: of whom I am chief.
-1 Timothy 1:15
(**The Apostle Paul viewed himself as a saint chief of preaching the gospel to sinners.)

In Closing

And they overcame him by the blood of the Lamb, and by the word of their testimony: and they loved not their lives unto the death. - Revelation 12:10

We are Saints Saved by Grace! That is part of our common testimony! Yesterday we were Sinners...Today we are Saints by The Blood of the Lamb! He has risen from the grave and is now on the right hand of The Father. His Spirit lives in us and we are saved!

Let no one convince you that you are a "Sinner saved by grace." If you have repented and received Jesus Christ as Lord and Savior, you are a Saint with a heavenly inheritance of Life, Joy and Hope in The Holy Ghost!

He that is unjust, let him be unjust still: and he who is filthy, let him be filthy still:
and he that is righteous, let him be righteous still:
and he that is holy, let him be holy still.
-Revelation 22:11

Index

Scriptures used throughout publication for your personal Study.

-Revelation 12:10
-Revelation 22:11

Notes

31410571R00018

Made in the USA
Charleston, SC
16 July 2014

"I'm sorry if that hurts you," she continued. "I just want to be clear so there are no misunderstandings."

Looking up at her, he asked, "How can you be so sure about how you feel? We haven't seen each other in a long time."

Vanessa said calmly, "That's right—we haven't seen each other in eighteen months. And that should tell you a lot about how I feel. You see, I know what *real love is*! And after all the pain I've known from losing the two most important people in my life, if I were still in love with you, nothing would have kept me away from you for so long—not even *anger*."

Craig looked uncomfortable as he said, "Yeah, well, speaking of anger, you unleashed a lot of it at me. I didn't know how to react when you called me the night of the accident. You surprised me and hurt me—ending our relationship so abruptly."

Vanessa said, "I know my phone call caught you by surprise. But just imagine my surprise when I got a phone call from the police about my parents' accident." Pausing she looked at Craig and said in a somewhat perplexed tone, "You had to have seen our breakup coming—we hadn't been happy together in months."

"Yeah, maybe so, but I was still hoping we could turn it around. But after you said it was over between us, I didn't know what else to do except give you some personal space to deal with your grief."

Craig's words irked Vanessa. Sitting back on the bench, she folded her arms across her chest and said sarcastically, "Well, gee, thanks for all the personal space to deal with my grief—how generous of you!"

Craig frowned, hurt by her snippy tone.

Today's about healing, not hurting, she thought. Vanessa tried again without the biting tone. "Don't you see? That's the point I was trying to make a few minutes ago. If you truly love someone, that's when you're supposed to show up. Even if the person tells you to go away, the love you feel—*if it's real*—will not let you just walk away. You'd find a way to keep reaching out, even if it's just by sending a card or a letter to let them know you're available when they're ready to talk. I didn't hear from you one time after the accident until just a few days ago."

Craig shifted uncomfortably in his seat, wrestling with his thoughts. After a long silence, he looked at her and said, "I'll be honest with you, Vanessa—I didn't feel emotionally strong enough back then to help you through your grief.

So when you said you didn't want to see me anymore, I took that as my way out." Pausing for a moment, he continued, "I made it all about me and not about you—and I'm really sorry for that! Your parents were always nice to me. I regret not going to their service, and not being available to you before now."

Vanessa was quiet for a few minutes, reflecting on Craig's confession and apology. Finally she said, "Well, you're not the only one with regrets. I apologize for the way I talked to you that night, trying to make you responsible for the accident. I was—"

Craig held up a hand to stop Vanessa. "No, whatever you do, please do not apologize to me for anything. I knew that was just the grief talking. But I do want to apologize for standing you up that day."

Vanessa had often wondered what prevented Craig from coming back early. And now, when she had the chance to ask, she took a pass, imagining that anything he would say would not be satisfactory. It was time to let go of all of this pain and disappointment.

Several quiet moments passed between them, as they fixed their gaze onto the people and scenery around them.

After a few minutes, Vanessa looked at Craig and said, "You know what I'd like to do?"

"What's that?"

"Keep moving forward—and not look back."

Craig took a deep breath. "I wish we could move forward together, but that's not going to happen, is it?"

There was a pause. Vanessa said, "We can as *friends*."

Joking to cut the blow, Craig winced. "Oh, no, please—not the 'let's be friends' speech."

Smiling at him, she said, "Okay, I'll skip the speech, *my friend*."

Craig returned the smile, knowing that Vanessa had just squashed any notions he had of them ever getting back together.

After a few more quiet moments, he asked, "So tell me, how are you doing these days—I mean *really* doing?"

Knowing that Craig was asking how she was coping with her grief, Vanessa said, "All I can say is that grief is a journey—a real trip! I feel stronger than I did three months ago. And three months ago, I was probably stronger than the previous three months. But when I allow myself to deeply think about losing my parents, the pain feels fresh all over again, like I'm right back to square one."

"Yeah, I can only imagine how it feels." Craig thought of his own parents—still physically well and active. "Have you considered grief counseling? It might be helpful."

Thinking of Elliott, Vanessa said, "You're the second person over the past few days to suggest it. I'm considering it. In the meantime, I stay busy, because it helps keep me in the present and out of the past, where my emotions tend to run high."

"I can understand that. And speaking of staying busy, I've got some news." Craig said. "I went back to work several months ago—as a controller for a medical membership association." He paused, looking for a reaction from Vanessa. Receiving none, he smiled and said, "I've temporarily parked my singing dreams—I've got bills to pay!"

Remembering how his career dreams had been the beginning of the end for them, she said, "Well, I wish you well with your dreams. I hope you remember I tried to be supportive."

"Yeah, I do. And I remember I didn't make it easy for you."

Seeing the regret in Craig's eyes, Vanessa said, "I want you to be happy."

"And I want the same for you."

"Thank you for the vase of pink tea roses. They're my favorite."

"Yeah, I know they are. And you're welcome."

Recognizing that nothing more needed to be said for a while, they sat back on the bench under a clear sky.

Chapter 12

The clock on Elliott's nightstand showed that it was 7:17 p.m. Stretched out on his king-size bed, he had awakened a few minutes earlier surprised to find that his short nap had turned into a two hour snooze.

Elliott's home was quiet this evening. After he and Nicole had finished touring the museum, he dropped her off to spend the night at her Aunt Evelyn's home. Evelyn was Elliott's sister and only sibling. She and her husband, Paul, had a daughter, Sonya, who was three months older than Nicole, and the girls were best friends. Nicole spent most Saturday nights with them.

In the first year following Lisa's death when everything had felt off-centered in Elliott's life, Evelyn had helped him, offering extra hands-on help and guidance with Nicole on little girl issues like hair, clothing, and more. And even now with Elliott having completely mastered the role of caring for his young daughter, he was still appreciative of his sister's ongoing support and that of his parents, who lived in Princeton, New Jersey. Both Nicole and Sonya spent two weeks during the summer every year with their grandparents.

Elliott got up from the bed and walked to the window, looking outside at nothing in particular for his thoughts were on Vanessa. He liked her relaxed, casual side; she had natural beauty. Her lips held a constant smile, and she was warm and gentle with Nicole. She had an aura of simplicity about her that he liked very much.

Wondering how Vanessa's afternoon had gone with her ex-fiancé, Elliott decided he needed to do something to take his mind off her. Reaching in his closet, he retrieved his briefcase and pulled out a printed draft of an article he was writing for a legal publication. As he reached for a pencil on the nightstand, the phone rang.

"Hello?" Elliott answered quickly, not bothering to check his caller ID box.

"Elliott—it's me, Vanessa."

Her voice was music to his ears. "Hey, I was just thinking about you."

"Good thoughts, I hope."

"Those are the only kind you've given me," he said with a smile. "What are you up to this evening?"

"I'm finally sitting down with my feet up, relaxing. After seeing Craig, I ran errands and then came home to do laundry and all of that other household stuff that's annoying but necessary."

Elliott smiled, thrilled that Vanessa had not spent all afternoon with Craig. "Well, I can relate. After the museum, I dropped Nicole off early at my sister's and ran some errands. I didn't realize how tired I was until I stretched out for thirty minutes and slept for two hours."

"A long nap sounds good," Vanessa said. "I just wanted to call and say thanks again for having me over this morning. I had a great time, and enjoyed meeting Nicole."

"Vanessa, we had a wonderful time with you, too." Elliott hesitated. Taking a deep breath, he asked, "So, how did things go this afternoon with Craig?"

Vanessa was glad Elliott asked, because she wanted him to know. "All things considered, it went well. I had been dreading the whole thing. We hadn't seen each other since before the accident, so it was a little awkward at first, but it ended okay. We said what we had to say, and can now move on."

"Move on?"

"Craig was hoping we might pick up where we left off, but that's not happening! We're going to work on being friends, although I seriously doubt that we'll see each other again anytime soon. But at least we parted amicably."

This was all good news to Elliott. "Well, of course, amicably is always best but not always possible."

"I apologized to Craig for trying to hold him accountable for the accident, and I have you to thank for helping me see the whole situation clearly."

"I believe you already knew it. Sometimes it just helps to hear someone else say it."

"Well, you've still been a blessing to me, Elliott. I hope you don't mind me saying that."

Elliott smiled. "No, I don't mind at all."

"Now before I say goodnight, I have an important question to ask you."

"Sure, what is it?"

"Would it be all right to invite myself over next Saturday for more pancakes?"

Elliott laughed. "Oh, I see, buttering me up for my pancakes, huh?"

"They were excellent." She chuckled. "And so was everything else!"

"Vanessa, we don't have to wait until next week. I can make pancakes again tomorrow morning. Or, to mix things up, I can make you a really good omelet."

"Be still my heart! I can't believe I know a man who can cook."

Elliott laughed again. "So, then, I take it you're coming over in the morning?"

"You bet!" Vanessa said, knowing she sounded eager, but was comfortable with it.

"Well, wait a second," Elliott said. He was thinking of an idea that had just popped in his head. "I think Sunday breakfast should come with a requirement."

"Okay, I'm listening."

"After serving you my world-famous omelet, how about joining me for worship service at my church?"

Vanessa smiled. "There's no way I can turn down an invitation to be fed both physically and spiritually."

"Amen to that, Vanessa."

"Well, I'll say goodnight, and see you tomorrow. Is 9 a.m. okay?"

"Yeah, it's fine. We'll have breakfast and leave for worship service around 10:30 a.m."

A few minutes later, they each hung up the phone, knowing that whatever this was going on between them, it was now moving full steam ahead.

Chapter 13

The next seven weeks flew by quickly with Elliott and Vanessa wasting no time falling head over heels for each other. In person and over the phone, they talked at length about everything under the sun. They discovered they had many things in common, and where they differed didn't matter enough to stop their relationship from moving forward.

When weekday evenings turned out to be too hectic to get together without feeling rushed, they blocked quality time on weekends, so they could leisurely enjoy each other's company. On Saturdays, Vanessa loved spending time with Elliott and Nicole at their home; on Sunday afternoons following worship, they all headed to Vanessa's place, allowing her to show off her culinary skills. And during the week, they burned up the text and FaceTime features on their cell phones—squeezing in a lunch when they could manage it, usually about twice a week.

It was now 8 a.m. on a very special Saturday in October. Tossing back the quilt that covered her, Vanessa turned over in bed, squinting to read the caller ID screen on her ringing phone. Seeing that it was Elliott, she smiled brightly.

Clearing the sleepy sound from her throat, Vanessa answered the phone cheerfully. "Good morning!"

"Good morning, Sweetheart. I would sing happy birthday to you, but I don't want to ruin your morning with my singing."

Lying back on the pillow, Vanessa pressed the phone close to her ear, wishing it was not separating them. "There's no way you can ruin my morning, especially after telling me that you love me!"

Eight hours earlier, Elliott had surprised Vanessa with a midnight phone call, wishing her a happy birthday and telling her that he was in love with her. His declaration had made her heart sing with joy because she was also in love with him. When she had asked if what they were feeling was all too much too quickly, he had chuckled and said, "Sweetie, if God could create the universe within one week, surely we can fall in love in seven weeks." She didn't see how she could argue against such sound reasoning.

"So, how are you feeling this morning?"

"I feel loved by you, and only one day older than yesterday."

Laughing, Elliott said, "Well, I'd say that your day is getting off to a good start."

"Can you still join me this morning for a bike ride?" They had biked along the National Mall a couple of Saturdays ago with plans to do it again on her birthday.

Hating to disappoint her, Elliott said, "I wish I could, but I have an emergency meeting in two hours with a client."

"No problem, we'll just do it another time. But I think I'll still get up and exercise; perhaps take a jog through my neighborhood."

"Well, enjoy your run, if that's what you decide to do. But please skip the music and earphones, so you can hear what's going on around you."

"Yes, sir. I will do that," Vanessa playfully responded.

"I know I sound overly protective, but I don't want anyone creeping up behind you."

"I don't either. I'll be careful, I promise."

"And I'm holding you to that promise."

"Honey, what time should I be ready this evening? And, by the way, you never did tell me where we're going or what we're doing."

Elliott smiled. "I'll pick you up at 5 p.m. sharp and dress to impress! And that's all you need to know for now."

Reflecting on the two new dresses that she had bought last week, Vanessa decided one of them would be perfect for tonight. "Well, I'll be ready. Hey, I hope your emergency meeting is resolved to your satisfaction."

"Thanks, that makes both of us. I'll call you in a few hours and put Nicole on the phone. I know she wants to wish you a happy birthday."

"Great! In the meantime, give her a big hug for me."

"You bet. Vanessa, I love you and I'll call you later."

"I love you, too!"

Fighting the urge to pull the covers over her shoulders and go back to sleep, Vanessa rolled out of bed and readied herself for her jog. Forty-five minutes later, she began a two-mile run through her neighborhood. Enjoying the chilly air and relatively quiet streets, she moved at a slower pace than usual, permitting herself to reminisce on past birthday celebrations with her parents. Her heart rejoiced and ached with every remembrance.

Ten minutes into running her regular route, Vanessa changed directions and started running up a steep hill. Pushing the hill with a stronger stride, her thoughts shifted to other areas of her life.

Thanks to Elliott's strong faith in God, Vanessa was following his lead, and she was back in the rhythm of regular Sunday worship. She was attending a Baptist church that he had joined about ten years ago, and on her own, she was seeking a Christian Bible study group for women of all denominations, because she liked learning from expansive and diverse conversations.

Vanessa's consulting business was thriving, but she wanted to do even more in the area of event planning. Her renewed vision was to not only manage the logistical flow of events, but to use her talents to collaborate with clients to conceptualize, write, and develop creative content for their event. She had a former colleague, now working as a creative producer for a large entertainment company, who was giving her solid advice on how to get moving in the area of creative content.

Ten minutes later, Vanessa turned onto her block. She was invigorated from her morning run. Feeling exceedingly happy on her birthday, she prayed inwardly, *God, thank you for allowing me to see another birthday. I thank you for bringing Elliott and Nicole into my life. I thank you for my relatives and friends, and for everything that supports me and gives me strength from day to day.*

At 5 p.m. sharp, Elliott rang the doorbell. Vanessa, who had lost track of time taking birthday phone calls from several friends, was running a few minutes late and still getting dressed. She opened the door and then darted back upstairs so quickly, he had only caught a glimpse of her wrapped in her robe, running up the steps. Elliott laughed and called out, "Slow down!"

Shortly after, Vanessa, now fully dressed, reached for her perfume bottle and sprayed a dab behind each ear. After taking a final look in the mirror, she headed downstairs feeling and looking beautiful.

"Sweetie, you take my breath away!" Elliott said, extending her his hand as she stepped off the bottom step.

"I'm glad you approve," she said, turning around to show off her purple satin party dress that complimented both her skin tone and her figure. An amethyst necklace, matching dangle earrings, and purple strappy heels completed her outfit.

"Oh, yeah, I definitely approve!" Elliott said leaning in to kiss Vanessa on the lips.

"You've got it going on too, Mr. Reeves!" Vanessa said, admiring the charcoal gray suit, white collared shirt and golden silk tie that he was wearing. "You look so handsome that you could make any of those Hollywood hunks run and hide."

Elliott chuckled. "That's what you say now, but I bet if any of those brothers walked in here, you'd pretend like you didn't know me."

Vanessa teased, "Well, I wouldn't pretend like I didn't know you. I would just pretend like I didn't know you *very well.*"

"Oh, so it's like that, is it?" Elliott teased right back, wrapping her in his arms. "I tell you that I love you, and you would pretend you don't know me well."

"You know I'm just teasing," Vanessa said sweetly, cuddling in his arms. "You're the only man for me!"

No more words were needed, as the look in their eyes said it all.

A moment later, Elliott snapped his finger as if he had forgotten something. He turned toward the front door. "Before we leave, I have a birthday present for you on the front porch."

The front porch?

Looking through a small window pane on the door, Elliott opened the door wide.

"Hey, girlfriend!" said Rita, stepping inside. She was wearing a beautiful grin on her brown, round, pretty, freckled face, and right behind her was Mike, looking equally happy.

"I can't believe my eyes!" Stepping forward, Vanessa threw her arms around Rita. "I think I'm going to cry!"

"That makes two of us!" Rita said, hugging Vanessa tightly. Rita, who was slightly taller than Vanessa and about ten pounds heavier, was wearing a black-and-white, wrap-style maxi dress and black heels.

Amused by the two women, Mike rolled his eyes. "Look now, y'all need to push the pause button on those tears. I know I speak for Elliott when I say that we don't have time to watch you all cry a bucket of tears, mess up your eye make-up, and then try to park us in a corner while you run off and reapply more."

"My brother, you keep it real!" Elliott chuckled.

"Yeah, man, I do. You've got to rein in Rita and Vanessa before they get out of control."

Laughing, Vanessa and Rita separated. Vanessa walked over and playfully punched Mike in the arm. "I'm glad to see you—even if you are a complete nut." She reached up and kissed him on the side of his cheek. Mike had a bald head and a stocky build. He was in his early forties, but when he smiled, he looked years younger. Tonight he was wearing a black suit, a white collared shirt, and a black-and-white tie. Vanessa wondered if Rita had pestered him to wear it, because suits were not his style.

Mike grinned at Vanessa and turned his face to the other side. "Now plant a kiss on this side, and I'll forget you just called me a nut."

With a big smile, Elliott stepped forward. "Okay, break it up. Mike doesn't need another kiss. Besides, where's mine?" he asked, looking at Vanessa. "I played a part in this surprise."

"Oh, I've got something extra special for you!" Vanessa said, reaching over and planting a deep smooch on Elliott's cheek, deliberately branding him with her lip color.

They all laughed.

"Hey, I'm tempted to not wipe it off," Elliott said, looking at himself in the mirror by the front door. "I should take a picture of it, in case I ever have to prove in a court of law that you're crazy about me."

Mike smiled. "Rita, it looks like we made a good match with these two."

"And we thank you!" Elliott said, as Vanessa gently wiped her lipstick color from his cheek.

Rita playfully rolled her eyes. "And just think—it almost didn't happen because of Vanessa's attitude. Elliott, she was *not* interested in meeting you."

Vanessa smiled. "You're never going to let me forget that, are you?"

"Nope, at least not any time soon."

Coming to Vanessa's defense, Elliott said, "Well, of course, I can't take it personally, because she didn't know me."

Turning to Vanessa, Rita smiled and said, "It must be nice having your own defense attorney speak for you."

"Girl, it's divine!" Vanessa chuckled, as Elliott slipped his arms around her waist and hugged her tightly.

"Well, I'm glad that you all are happy together," Mike said with a big grin. "Now let's roll on out of here. I'm ready to get my grub on. I'm in the mood for both steak and lobster."

Rita gave Mike a look of disbelief. "You want steak *and* lobster? Don't forget that we are dinner guests tonight. Try not to order everything on the menu."

Smiling, Elliott intervened and said, "You all are my guests. Please order whatever you like on the menu—and as much of it as you want."

"Thank you, my brother," Mike said with a slight bow. "And when you and Vanessa come back to New York, I'll treat you all to a very special dinner." Then, looking at Rita, "You, on the other hand, can pay for your own dinner," he joked.

They all laughed.

Elliott walked toward the front door. "Come on, Mike, I think I need to get you out of here before you get yourself into some real trouble with Rita."

Mike chuckled and said, "Yeah, that's probably a good idea!"

"I agree!" Rita laughed. The men headed out to the car with Rita calling out to them, "We'll be out in a few minutes. I need to catch up with my girl!"

"Rita, honestly, I'm surprised you kept all of this a secret from me," Vanessa said, giving her best friend another hug. "When did Elliott call and invite you guys down?"

"Last weekend. He said he wanted to make your birthday extra special. Girl, that man is in *love*! And from the looks of you, you are, too!"

Smiling, Vanessa said, "Well, since you are so observant, how come you haven't said anything about my new dress?"

"Because I'm too busy watching cupid fly all around your head with his love arrow."

Vanessa chuckled. "Rita, you're too much!"

Then, changing the subject, Vanessa asked, "What time did you all get in today?"

"We arrived at Elliott's around noon. He's got a beautiful home! Who's his decorator?"

"He gives all decorating credit to his late wife, Lisa. She was a history professor, but interior decorating was her hobby."

"Oh, I see," said Rita. "Hey, I met Nicole who is just as sweet as you said."

Vanessa smiled. "Yeah, she's a sweetheart. So, how long are you and Mike staying?"

"We're leaving after tomorrow's game."

Vanessa looked surprised. "You're going to the game with us?"

Rita grinned. "We sure are! Elliott has tickets for all of us, including Nicole. And, girl, Washington had better beat those Cowboys!"

Vanessa laughed. "We'll have to pray about that on the way to the game! In the meantime, let's get going—our men are patiently waiting for us."

"Wait a minute." Rita turned Vanessa toward her and looked her right in the eye. "All kidding aside, I wish you a beautiful birthday, my sister, and a blessed new year ahead."

Taking Rita by the hand, Vanessa said, "Thanks, Sis! I'm so glad you and Mike are here."

The two stepped out onto the front porch. Rita, noting that Mike was standing near the front passenger door of Elliott's car, called out, "Mike, don't you even think about sitting up front with Elliott. You get in the back with me!"

"Well, excuse me!" Mike grinned. "I thought you two wanted to sit together and continue talking behind our backs."

Rita said, "Well, you thought wrong!" She turned back to Vanessa, who was locking the front door. "We may have issues to work out, but I love *that man*."

Vanessa locked arms with Rita. "I know you do. You two are going to work it out. Now let's go have some fun!"

Chapter 14

A week later, Vanessa entered Moses Baptist Church—where she attends worship service with Elliott. He had surprised her with a gift certificate for a five-week grief counseling course offered by the counseling ministry there. The last course for the year was beginning today at 6 p.m.

When Elliott handed the certificate to Vanessa, he told her there was no expiration date on it and to use it whenever she was ready. And today she was ready—especially now that she was planning her quarterly trip to Richmond next week to check on the family property. Previous trips had only been for the day, but this time she was spending a few nights to take care of some administrative and household matters. It was a trip she knew would be emotional for her, and Elliott also knew it.

Vanessa had arrived early for the first meeting, hoping for a few minutes alone to relax and organize her thoughts. Looking around the cheerfully decorated meeting room, her eyes settled on a colorful poster with a beautiful scene of a crystal blue lake surrounded by trees and a field of red tulips. Written in white letters within the blue lake were the following words: "It may seem impossible now, but the little things you remember will help you push forward, smile again, and fully embrace life." Studying the print, Vanessa thought, *Thankfully, I now know that to be true.*

Moments later, the door opened and in walked a tall, young woman about thirty with a dark complexion and a head of thick cornrow braids. Following closely on her heels were three older women in their sixties. Based on their chatter, Vanessa observed that they were fairly acquainted with each other.

After everyone sat down at the table and got comfortable, the younger woman walked to the front of the room. With a warm smile, she said, "Good evening, everyone! My name is Regina Adams, and I'm a ministry leader trained in bereavement counseling."

Pausing to look around the table, she continued, "As we know, bereavement refers to the loss of a loved one, but can also refer to other types of life events. Over the next five weeks, I'll be leading you through discussions on the loss of loved ones and the five stages of grief." Using her fingers, she counted off each stage, "Denial, anger, bargaining with God, depression, and acceptance."

I don't know what I'm getting myself into here, Vanessa thought. *I pray it'll be all right!*

Regina continued, "Bereavement is a normal and complex process. We all know that the pain of losing someone we love can be overwhelming—our thoughts and feelings can run wild. But it's important to acknowledge the pain and be willing to face it. So I applaud each of you for taking this course, wanting to deepen your understanding about what it is you feel, so you can learn how to accept it without feeling the need to shut yourself down in pain. It's my hope that over the next several weeks, we'll freely converse with each other, help each other, and learn from each other. So before we begin, let's all briefly introduce ourselves ..."

A short while later, Regina continued, "Before we begin tonight's discussion, it's important to know several things. First, we all experience grief in our own unique way. Not everyone goes through all five stages of grief—and very rarely does anyone go through the stages in a prearranged order."

Looking at Regina, Vanessa thought, *I can attest to that—I skipped over denial and went straight to anger.*

"The stages of grief are a mixture of thoughts and emotions. You can move from one stage to the next—and back and forth."

"I can certainly speak about denial!" Ethel, who was seated next to Vanessa, announced.

"And we want you to tell us about it," Regina said, looking warmly at Ethel. "But first, let me explain denial so that we all understand it."

Looking around, Regina connected with each member of the class—Vanessa, Ethel, Aretha and Ruby—before she continued, "Denial helps us unconsciously manage what we're feeling. And the way it affects us is almost always short-term, passing us through the first wave of sorrow."

Turning to Ethel, Regina said, "You can go ahead now and share your experience."

After taking a sip of water to clear her throat, Ethel said, "My son, Ricky, died six months ago in a boating accident in Florida. In the first few weeks following his death, somehow my thoughts shifted and I stopped thinking of him as being dead—even though I had seen his body and planned his funeral." She paused a moment. "You see, Ricky traveled a lot for his job, so I just allowed myself to imagine him on one of those business trips he was always going on. Thinking of him as traveling kept me calm." Turning to the others, she asked, "Now, is that not the strangest thing ever? To think my son is on a pleasurable trip when he's dead?"

If that's strange, then call me strange, too! Vanessa thought, remembering the brief time she had allowed herself to envision her parents on a nice trip somewhere, because the reality of their death was too hard to accept.

"Ethel, it's not strange at all. What you experienced is a form of denial," said Regina. Turning to the rest of the class, she said, "Denial will have some people thinking their loved ones are on a journey and simply unreachable for a period of time. But denial can also distract your thought process, leading you to focus keenly on the circumstances surrounding the way your loved one died."

Once again, Ethel spoke up and said, "That's true! I questioned everything about the accident. The process of asking questions and investigating kept my mind busy and helped me manage my sorrow." Pausing a moment, she stated, "There were days when I focused less on Ricky's physical absence, and more on the circumstances surrounding his accident. And as strange as this might sound, it helped me get through the day."

Vanessa said softly, "Denial sounds like a blessing in disguise."

"In a way, it is, Vanessa," said Regina. "It's a blessing in that it allows us to pace our feelings. But it's not a good place to be permanently. Would you like to share your personal experience, if any, with denial?"

Taking a few moments to consider what she wanted to share, Vanessa began, "My parents were killed in a car crash in Virginia. Once I settled their affairs, I couldn't leave Richmond fast enough. Here, I can walk down the street and not be reminded that the bakery on the corner is where Mom bought the lemon chiffon cakes she was so crazy about. Or drive by the barbershop where Dad always got his hair cut. Rushing back to DC was my way of escaping my new reality." Vanessa looked over at Regina. "But in the end, it didn't help. You can't get away from what's inside of you."

"Thank you for sharing, Vanessa, and I'm deeply sorry for the loss of your parents."

Vanessa nodded.

"Does anyone else want to share their experience with denial?"

With hands going up, Vanessa sat back relieved to have the spotlight shift somewhere else.

Aretha said, "When my mom died seven months ago, I told all of her close friends. But later on—I'm talking weeks after her funeral—I remembered there were a lot of other people that I simply forgot to notify. People like her manicurist and hair stylist and a few others. And when I thought about calling to tell them, I just couldn't say the words 'My mom died.' So I just never told them. For all they know, she just has never been back to see them."

Vanessa asked, "Now that some time has passed, do you feel stronger? Do you think you could call these people today and tell them that your mom passed away?"

Aretha thoughtfully reflected on Vanessa's question. "Yeah, I think I'm somewhat stronger, and maybe I could make those phone calls. But, of course, you know what'll happen when I do—they'll express their sympathy and tell me what a great mother I had. And while it's nice to hear all of that, it'll just leave me feeling depressed all over again. Therefore, I think I'm just going to let it be for a while."

Ruby said slowly, "Yeah...that's a good idea...to just let it all be!" She wiped her eyes, fighting back tears. "Ever since my twin sister died, I've let a whole lot of things just be. Rhonda and I were extremely close, as I suppose most twins are, and her death left a giant whole in my life. I didn't know how to be me anymore without her. We still went shopping together most weekends, sometimes buying the same outfits just for the sheer fun of it. We enjoyed each other—and laughed a lot. And when she died six months ago, I stopped laughing."

Without saying a word, Regina reached over and placed a box of tissues in the center of the table. One by one, all the women reached forward and plucked a handful to wipe away the tears falling from their eyes. Their tears fell for Ruby but mostly for themselves.

About thirty minutes later, Regina slowly wrapped up the tender stories and testimonies. She passed out grief journals, encouraging everyone to use them between classes to capture their thoughts and emotions. "As a reminder," she said in closing, "next week's session topic will cover the anger stage of grief."

I know all about that one, Vanessa thought. *I was angry with God, Craig, and myself.*

Vanessa raised her hand. "Regina, I'll miss next week's class because I'll be out of town."

"That's not a problem, Vanessa. If you like, we can meet separately when you're back."

"Thanks. I appreciate it!"

Vanessa was the first to exit the meeting room. Turning the corner in the hallway, she was pleasantly surprised to see Elliott standing near the entrance of the sanctuary. They had talked earlier in the day, but had made no plans to see each other this evening.

Walking quickly toward him, Vanessa smiled and said, "Honey, what are you doing here?"

Elliott looked at her thoughtfully. "I wanted to come by and see you," he said, opening his arms to embrace her. "I thought you might need a hug—and after the long day I've had, I know I need my arms around you."

Vanessa smiled, leaning into Elliott and wrapping her arms around his waist.

Elliott leaned down and kissed Vanessa on her forehead. "How was your class?"

With her head resting on his chest, she sighed. "I can best sum it up in two words—emotional and enlightening."

Elliott nodded. "One of the benefits of group counseling is that you find out you're not alone in what you're going through."

"That's for sure—everyone feels the sting of death." Looking up at Elliott, she said, "Thanks for signing me up for the classes. I think they're going to really help me."

"Sweetie, I think so, too."

"Hey, wait a minute," Vanessa said leaning back from his arms and looking around. "Where's Nicole?"

"Don't worry, she's fine. She's in the sanctuary waiting for me to hurry back and rescue her."

Vanessa looked perplexed. "Rescue her from what?"

Elliott smiled. "The youth choir is rehearsing tonight, and the director's trying hard to recruit Nicole."

"Is she interested in singing?"

Shaking his head, Elliott said, "No, she's not. Nicole's in enough activities for now, and every activity she's in means that I'm in it, too."

Vanessa chuckled lightly. "Hey, if our girl needs rescuing, let's go get her!"

Elliott smiled at Vanessa's reference to Nicole as 'our girl.' Looking down into her eyes, he thought, *God, thank you for bringing Vanessa into my life and giving her a heart big enough to fully embrace me and my daughter!*

Chapter 15

At DC's busy Union Station, a long passenger line had already formed at the gate for the train to Richmond that was leaving at 7:30 a.m.

Initially, Vanessa had planned to drive, but Elliott had suggested she take the train to arrive feeling relaxed. He had wanted to go with her, but was overseeing an important case getting underway this afternoon in Superior Court. He was planning to drive to Richmond on Saturday, along with Nicole, to pick Vanessa up and bring her back. In the meantime, he was glad that Vanessa's Uncle Ray and Aunt Rachel were driving to Richmond to be with her for a few days.

As an Amtrak attendant prepared to open the gate, Vanessa turned to face Elliott. Taking her into his arms, he held her in a long embrace. Finally looking up at him, she smiled and whispered, "You do know that I'll see you in a few days, right?"

"Yes, I do," he whispered back. "I thought I'd give you something to remember me by."

With a smile, Vanessa said, "Trust me, I could never forget you."

Cupping her chin in his hand, he said, "I hope you know how much I love you."

"I do, and I love you, too!"

Elliott kissed her lightly. "Have a blessed trip. I'll call you this evening."

With the departure gate now open, Vanessa and Elliott inched forward in line, nearing the point where they would have to separate. As Vanessa approached the agent, she held up her ticket for inspection, and the agent waved her through the gate. Inside the walkway, she turned and looked through the glass, blowing a kiss to Elliott. Smiling, he waved at her and inwardly prayed, *Lord, please strengthen Vanessa as she journeys back home. Guide her and protect her!*

Vanessa boarded the Quiet Car. It was practically empty, allowing her the seat of her choice. She moved toward the middle and took a seat by the window. Once the train left the station, she removed a new paperback book from her bag and dozed off before finishing the first chapter.

The train arrived in Richmond two hours and forty minutes later. Vanessa collected her suitcase, exited the train station on Main Street, and caught a taxi. The ride through the streets of her home city brought back so many touching memories. Autumn was Vanessa's favorite season, so she refocused her attention onto the colorful trees that lined the streets along the route home. When the taxi pulled up in the drive way of her Garrison-style family home, her breathing rhythm had rapidly increased.

Why didn't I ask Gladys to meet me here? Vanessa thought. Gladys Jones was a highly trusted family friend living two miles away. She had a key to the house and the auxiliary code to the alarm system. Vanessa had hired Gladys to stop by the house weekly to handle some light dusting, arrange for yard care, and to ensure that all was well. Vanessa was considering installing a new home security system that would allow her to monitor the home from DC, using her computer.

Vanessa also stayed in touch with several neighbors—they kept her abreast of changes in the neighborhood. Sooner or later, she knew she would have to make a decision about this home. And the choices were obvious: keep it as a vacation home, rent it, or put it up for sale.

Entering the home and disarming the alarm system, Vanessa shut the door and placed her suitcase beside it. She sat her shoulder bag on the table in the foyer. The silence inside was unbearably loud. All she could feel was the absence of her parents.

Her arms crossed, self-protectively, Vanessa wandered through the house. As she stood in the living room, she could see straight into the dining room. Glancing to her right, she looked up the winding staircase, leading to the four bedrooms. The home was in excellent condition, looking basically the same as it always had, with drapes at the windows, art on the walls, and furniture in all the rooms. All clothing had been removed from closets and drawers and disbursed between family, friends, and charitable groups. Vanessa had moved all documents, valuable treasures, and sentimental items to her home in DC.

Taking a seat on the couch, the memories of growing up in this house with her parents began to stir. Vanessa buried her face into her hands. *This is too much for me!* She got down on her knees, and in a trembling voice, closed her eyes, intending to pray. But instead, she sank down on the carpeted floor and wept. In between her sobs, she whispered, "God, I'd give anything if you'd allow me to see, with my own eyes, a glimpse of my mother and father. I just need to see for myself that they're all right."

After Vanessa's tears subsided, she thought back on the request she had made to God to see her parents and shook her head in disbelief. *I think I just experienced the stage of grief where you try to bargain with God. Like that's even possible.* She pulled herself up from the floor and sat back down on the couch, wiping her tear-stained face.

After a while, Vanessa stood up feeling stronger. *I need to wake up this house,* she thought. Finding a radio, she turned it on and switched the dial to a contemporary Christian station. The lyrics and the upbeat melody of songs lifted Vanessa's spirit. She willed herself to stay encouraged. Her uncle and aunt were driving to Richmond to be with her, and she wanted to be strong for them. Having just finished a long and therapeutic cry, she hoped she had extracted enough sadness to make it through the next few days without another emotional collapse.

Vanessa made a list of things to do, with grocery shopping at the top of the list. After refreshing her appearance, she grabbed her shoulder bag, and headed to the garage. Her mother's favorite car was an old classic VW Beetle. Retrieving the key, Vanessa prayed the car would start—and have enough gas to get her to the store. As she turned the ignition, the car made an awful cranking noise. Taking a deep breath, Vanessa whispered, "Come on, baby." Turning the key again, the engine complied. Looking at the gas gauge, Vanessa estimated there was enough in the tank to get to the nearest gas station two miles away. After pushing the button on the automatic garage door opener, she put the car in drive. Looking again at the gas gauge, she thought, *God, come take a ride with me!*

An hour later, Vanessa arrived home with groceries and several bouquets of pink carnations. After putting the groceries away and the carnations into vases, Vanessa changed into sweatpants and a t-shirt and embarked on a cleaning marathon. She vacuumed all the rugs, ran the dust mop over the hardwood floors and a duster over all the tables. To her delight, there was little dust to collect, and that was solid proof to her that Gladys was on top of the dusting.

Vanessa changed the linen in the guest bedroom and put a vase of carnations on top of the dresser. After spraying the entire home with a lemon-scent air neutralizer, she sat down feeling exhausted. *That's all for now—I need to shower, get dressed, and put on a positive face. Uncle Ray and Aunt Rachel should be here within the hour.*

Chapter 16

Vanessa stood at the living room window, looking down the street where she grew up, wondering where some of her childhood friends might be today—especially her old friend, Vickie. Over many long, hot summer days, they had spent hours jumping rope, roller skating, riding bikes, and chasing lightning bugs at dusk. They were friends from the fourth through ninth grades, but lost contact when Vickie's parents divorced and she moved with her mother to Salisbury, North Carolina.

"Good morning, darling," said Aunt Rachel, as she slowly ascended the stairs. She and Uncle Ray had arrived yesterday afternoon. Vanessa had warmly welcomed them and had treated them to dinner last night at a new seafood restaurant.

Smiling at the sound of her aunt's voice, Vanessa turned away from the window, walking briskly over to the stairs. "Good morning, Aunt Rachel. I hope you and Uncle slept well last night." She extended her hand to help her aunt step down safely from the last step.

Aunt Rachel chuckled. "Yes, honey, I slept well—in spite of your uncle's loud snoring."

Giving her aunt a hug, Vanessa laughed and said, "Is that what that noise was? I thought an old frog had gotten in the house."

"Hey, who are you calling an old frog?" a crackly baritone voice rumbled from the top of the staircase.

Startled by the heavy pitch of his voice, Vanessa jumped, making her uncle laugh.

Feigning frustration, Vanessa said, "Uncle, you scared the daylights out of me!"

He laughed. "Well, that's good. That'll teach you to talk about people behind their back."

Aunt Rachel laughed as she made her way to the kitchen for a cup of coffee.

Vanessa watched her uncle descend the stairs. Despite his fragile health, at seventy-three, he was still a strong built man with a distinguished presence. *He looks so much like my dad*, she thought. Smiling at him, she willed herself to stay strong. Her uncle sensed what she was thinking. After he stepped all the way down, he opened his arms to offer her a hug and she gladly accepted it. After their therapeutic hug, she said, "I've got your favorite coffee brewing."

He took a big sniff of the air and sighed happily. "You're spoiling me."

Vanessa grinned. "What would you and Aunt Rachel like for breakfast? I can make a big, heart-healthy pot of oatmeal, or fix eggs and turkey bacon."

"Hmmm, let me think," he said, enjoying all the pampering from his favorite niece. As they locked arms and headed to the kitchen, he said, "Let's skip the oatmeal and go with eggs and bacon this morning."

Vanessa felt grateful for this time with her uncle and aunt. Knowing that life is precious and fleeting, she wanted to pamper them, for they had been so extra-comforting to her since losing her parents. She was looking forward to introducing them to Elliott and Nicole on Saturday.

Walking down the hall to his corner office, Elliott was feeling tired and a little irritable after a long day in court with his client listening to critical testimony from a prosecution witness. As a senior partner, Elliott preferred managing the firm's business affairs. But every now and then, he'd take on a high-status case that required his level of expertise. And this was one of those cases.

Entering his spacious office, Elliott closed the door and lightly tossed his briefcase on the table under the large window overlooking Pennsylvania Avenue. Removing his suit jacket and placing it on a hanger behind the door, his thoughts lingered on today's courtroom activities and the shady testimony from the prosecution witness. Elliott knew the man was lying under oath—and now it was his job to make sure the jury knew it, too.

Sitting back in his chair and wearily rubbing his eyes, it took no time for Elliot's thoughts to shift to Vanessa, whose absence was also contributing to his low mood. They didn't visit each other every day, but liked knowing that they could, if they wanted to. Now, she was over a hundred plus miles away, and he couldn't wait for Saturday to drive to Richmond and bring her back. A short while ago, while still in court, he received a lovable text message from her. Now, reaching for his cell phone, he read her message again. And it made him smile again.

Glancing at the clock, Elliott saw where he had a full hour before he had to leave to pick up Nicole from school. Since he needed to work longer this evening to prepare for another day in court, his plan was to pick her up, place a take-out order from one of the nearby restaurants, and bring her back to the office with him. Fortunately, he did not have to bring Nicole to his office too often, but when he did, she absolutely loved it—enjoying the attention she got from his staff, playing games on his big computer screen, and trying new food delicacies from restaurants.

Picking up the phone, Elliott buzzed his secretary, Millie.

"Yes, Elliott?" she asked gingerly.

"I need you to round up my trial team—have them meet me in the conference room in fifteen minutes. And tell them they'll be working late tonight."

Oh, no! Millie thought. *Wonder if that goes for me, too?*

As if reading her mind, Elliott smiled. "Don't worry, Millie. You can leave on time, but the team is on lock-down for a few hours."

Picking up the phone a few minutes later, Elliott punched in Vanessa's cell phone number. Because he had been in court all day, they had only communicated through short text messages. But now he wanted to directly connect and hear his sweetheart's voice. He knew talking with Vanessa would rejuvenate his spirit for the long evening ahead.

Chapter 17

Vanessa stood at the kitchen counter, making a cup of steaming chamomile tea. Raising her voice to be heard over the blaring television, she called out, "Can I bring either of you anything?"

Aunt Rachel called back, "No, honey, just bring yourself in here, and sit down."

Vanessa chuckled. "I'll be there in a minute." She added sugar to her tea, grabbed an oatmeal cookie and a napkin, and carried them into the living room.

Vanessa plopped herself down on the couch next to Aunt Rachel, who was struggling to stay awake through the Friday edition of Dateline. Uncle Ray was already in a snoozing position in the oversized recliner. His eyes were closed.

Aunt Rachel patted her hand. "Honey, I'm glad to see you finally sit down today. You've been so busy. Did you accomplish all you wanted to do?"

"Yeah, pretty much," Vanessa said, sipping her tea. Over the last several days she had checked off numerous items on her to-do list. She'd put her mom's car in the shop for service, finished clearing out the garage, and carried several boxes of non-valuable knickknacks to Goodwill. She'd wiped down all the windows inside the house, while a window-cleaning crew washed them on the outside. A gutter-cleaning company had removed fallen leaves and installed a new gutter shield. And just a few hours ago, she had guided the gardener in trimming the hedges that circled the front porch.

Aunt Rachel asked, "When do you think you'll come back again?"

"I was wondering that myself earlier today. I need to check my schedule—but possibly in January, maybe the Martin Luther King holiday weekend." *I'd love for Elliott and Nicole to come with me*, she thought.

"I've been watching you the past several days, and I think you've done incredibly well handling all the emotions you must be feeling, being here at home."

"Well, if I'm managing well it's because you're both here with me. But Tuesday was a tough day. Stepping inside and knowing that Mom and Dad weren't here—and never will be again—was just a horribly sad and empty experience. I just wanted to run away, but where do I run?"

Reaching over and lightly rubbing Vanessa's shoulder, Aunt Rachel said softly, "You run right into the arms of Jesus!"

Proving that not every shut eye is asleep, Uncle Ray opened his and said, "Hallelujah and Amen to that!" He turned and looked at Vanessa. "But I know how you feel. Driving up and parking outside—knowing your parents weren't inside—made me sad, too. But then you opened the front door, my beautiful niece, and I felt calm all over, because I saw the best of them that lives on in you."

Vanessa said quietly, "Thank you."

"I'm only saying what's true."

Aunt Rachel said, "Tell us about these bereavement classes you're taking. Are they helping?"

Taking another sip of tea, Vanessa leaned forward and placed her cup on a coaster. "Well, I've only been to one class, but already it's helping me understand that what I feel is perfectly normal. And, hopefully, it will help me manage—or at least be more at ease —with the sad and helpless feelings that creep up from time to time."

Uncle Ray asked, "Is Christianity being discussed in these classes?"

"It didn't come up at the first class, but I suspect it might since the course is offered through a ministry at a Christian church. The second class was yesterday, but I'll catch up on it next week."

"What stage of grief was covered this week?" he wanted to know.

"Anger. We both know that I'm very familiar with that stage," Vanessa said. "Prayerfully, it's behind me now. I held on to it way too long."

Aunt Rachel nodded, understandingly.

"Well, I hope you all do discuss Christianity," Uncle Ray said. "I know all about grief counseling. And I know that when the classes are over, having a strong faith in God is the key to keep moving forward."

"Trust me, Uncle, I know that." *At least now I do!* Vanessa thought. "So how do you preach Christianity to nonbelievers who are dealing with grief?"

"Oh, that's easy," Uncle Ray said. "Don't preach! Just talk casually about it. Talking about God and the afterlife with a nonbeliever and answering questions might lead that person to believe in Christ one day. But the last thing you want to do is be aggressive, especially during a time when people are emotionally vulnerable."

"That's right," Aunt Rachel said. "Grief is a real bear to tackle, and adjusting to the loss of a loved one is difficult enough. But if there's an opportunity to make a case for Christianity and you have the person's full attention and willingness to listen, then certainly make the case."

Pausing for a moment to reflect, Uncle Ray said, "Whenever I counseled members of my church on their challenging situations, including grief, I required them to read and meditate on Psalm 23, because it's a very calming passage."

"Yes, it is," Vanessa said quietly, remembering that it was her mother's favorite psalm.

Uncle Ray continued on, "It's a glorious and resilient passage that assures us we have a mighty God in Heaven, who supplies all of our needs. Always hold Psalm 23 close to your heart, Vanessa. It'll give you strength to walk through every situation in your life."

Aunt Rachel added, "I know it gets difficult, dear, but just remember that your parents were Christians and their souls are resting peacefully with a God who loves them deeply. They're perfectly fine in His presence, and that's something you can firmly believe."

Vanessa nodded.

Looking over at Vanessa and smiling, Uncle Ray said, "Now, switching gears in this conversation, I want to hear some more about this man that's driving here tomorrow morning to pick you up."

The thought of Elliott made Vanessa smile. They had talked a long time last night, sharing details of their day. "Well, Elliott will be here tomorrow and you'll have the opportunity to meet him for yourself."

Looking at her husband, Aunt Rachel said, "I hope you don't get overly personal with Elliott. People don't like twenty questions right off the bat."

Chuckling, Vanessa said, "He's an attorney, so he knows how to object if you get personal too quickly."

"And if he objects, can I overrule him?"

Vanessa laughed. "Yes, Uncle, you can certainly try."

"Remind me again, what kind of law does Elliott practice?"

"The firm handles contract, criminal, and civil law."

Uncle Ray chuckled. "With crime the way it is, and people suing over any and every little thing, Elliott and his colleagues must be very busy and very wealthy!"

Playfully shaking her finger at her husband, Aunt Rachel said, "See, that's a perfect example of what not to say when you meet him tomorrow! Ray, you promise me right now that you'll not ask him about his income."

Uncle Ray playfully rolled his eyes. "Come on now, you've got to know that I wouldn't ask the man a question like that."

Vanessa, who already knew Elliott's substantial income, thought, *Uncle Ray, the answer would knock your socks off.*

"I know we'll meet Elliott tomorrow, but tell us why he's so special to you."

Vanessa smiled while thinking of how much to share about the man she had so quickly and easily fallen in love with. "Elliott has brightened my life, giving me so many reasons to feel happy and hopeful. He's intelligent, personable, and compassionate. And what's even better than all of that is his steadfast faith in God and devotion to his daughter."

Aunt Rachel smiled and asked, "How do you get along with Elliott's daughter?"

Thinking of all the goodness inside Nicole, Vanessa said, "Nicole and I are bonding well. She's a sweet child and very smart. Every now and then I catch her looking at me curiously, and I wonder what she's thinking, but then she'll flash that adorable smile of hers at me and it melts my heart. I feel bad that she lost her mother at such a young age."

"Yeah, I know what you mean," Aunt Rachel sighed softly. "But it's not easy at any age. So, tell me, do you really believe Elliott is *the one* for you?"

Nodding her head emphatically, Vanessa smiled. "Yes, Aunt Rachel, I do! Elliott and I believe that God put us on the path to meet and fall in love. And we don't want to disappoint Him. God is awesome, isn't he?"

Uncle Ray and Aunt Rachel looked at each other and turned back to Vanessa. Almost in unison, they asked, "Who you telling?"

Vanessa laughed. Slowly standing to her feet, she said, "I think I'll leave you two senior citizens alone to fall asleep watching the rest of Dateline. I'm going upstairs to stretch out and watch a movie."

Happy for their niece, Uncle Ray and Aunt Rachel playfully waved her out of the room.

When Vanessa disappeared up the stairs, Rachel turned to her husband and said, "Brand new love is so sweet and exciting. But you know what?"

Uncle Ray raised his brow.

"Old love—like ours—is just as thrilling!"

Winking his eye, Uncle Ray replied, "Baby, who you telling?"

Upstairs, Vanessa, tuckered out from her busy day, fell into a deep sleep.

Hours later, she awoke to the smell of coffee brewing. The radio was on, and joyful gospel music wafted through the air. Vanessa stretched and sat up, feeling buoyant and free, almost as if transported back in time to her years as a teenager.

The golden rays of the sun streamed into her old bedroom. Arising, she walked to the window to look out at the glorious day. She was surprised to see Elliott, with Nicole beside him in the passenger seat, pulling into the driveway. She hadn't expected them so early. Waving her hand to greet them, she hurried downstairs to tell her aunt and uncle they had arrived.

When Vanessa entered the kitchen, Aunt Rachel was standing with her back to her, looking out the window. Uncle Ray was only partly visible, because he was standing on the other side of the open refrigerator door.

"Good morning!" Vanessa sang out to them. "Elliott and Nicole surprised me and came early!" Her uncle and aunt turned in her direction. Suddenly, Vanessa felt tingly all over. She was not looking at Uncle Ray's and Aunt Rachel's faces. She was looking at those of her father and mother. Her mother's face glowed with happiness as she said, "Vanessa, we're so happy for you!" "He's a good man, baby," her father said with a wide grin. "We know all about him and his child."

With a gasp, Vanessa awakened from her dream and sat up in the bed. She glanced at the illuminated clock on the table. It was 3 a.m. As she took deep breaths to calm her beating heart, she reached for the remote control, turning on the television and lowering the volume so as not to wake her aunt and uncle. *It's only a dream*, she thought as she fluffed her pillows, resting back against them. *But I'm too jittery to go back to sleep!*

Only she did, drifting off minutes later.

Vanessa woke to the buzzing sound of her alarm clock, telling her it was 7 a.m. Fumbling, she reached over and turned it off. An infomercial was on the television screen, but the volume was low.

Concentrating hard, Vanessa thought of the dream that had awakened her a few hours earlier. She recalled her parents' glowing, smiling faces and comments about Elliott. This was not the first time her parents had appeared in her dreams, but it was the first time here in the family home. In the first few months after the accident, her parents had weaved in and out of multiple dreams without conversation, yet always appearing to be at peace and offering her something tender: a sweet smile, a hand-blown kiss, a friendly wave from a distance.

Resting back against the pillows, Vanessa pulled the bed covers up around her and prayed inwardly. *God, when I arrived here, I asked you to let me see my parents and you did in the only way possible right now— through my dreams. You've shown me more than once that they're all right and now I firmly believe it. I thank you for answering my prayers and for loving me even when I doubted you. Thank you for your never ending patience with me.*

Three hours later, Vanessa looked out the living room window and saw Elliott parking his car in the driveway. This time it was not a dream, even though Vanessa felt it could be—with her knight in a shining black Mercedes Sedan—there to scoop her up and whisk her away. Grabbing a sweater from the closet, Vanessa put it on quickly and opened the front door.

Emerging from the driver's side of the car, Elliott stood still, savoring the sight of Vanessa hurrying over to him. Opening his arms, she ran into them. As they squeezed each other tight, Nicole climbed out of the passenger side and ran over to them. "Come here, girlfriend," Vanessa said with a big smile, reaching down and taking Nicole into her arms.

Uncle Ray and Aunt Rachel watched the trio's display of affection, as they looked at them from behind the curtains at the living room window.

Aunt Rachel said, "Our girl is sure enough in love!"

Uncle Ray replied, "I'd say they all are!" He turned from the window. "Come on, baby, let's give those young folks some privacy," he said, adding joyfully, "I just know that Frank and Gloria are smiling from Heaven to see Vanessa happy and in love with people who love her right back!"

Chapter 18

On a sunny and cold Saturday afternoon two weeks before Christmas, Vanessa was about to introduce Nicole to the fine art of scrapbooking. The idea had come to her the previous weekend when she had helped Nicole decorate their Christmas tree, using ornaments that Lisa had painted for her daughter some years earlier. As Vanessa admired one of the ornaments, she had commented, "Your mother was very artistic!" Nicole had whispered, "Some days I can't remember her well." It was a sentiment that touched Vanessa's heart. Leaning down, she had kissed Nicole on the forehead and said, "Sweetie, I'll try to help you remember."

Mulling it over, Vanessa had decided on a scrapbook—Nicole's very own special mommy scrapbook, something she could pull out whenever she needed to emotionally connect with her mother. Vanessa had asked Elliott if it would be all right if she helped Nicole create it. He had liked the idea very much, but had asked Vanessa to do her best to make the project a positive experience. He wanted Nicole to be as happy as possible, especially with Christmas approaching. It was his favorite holiday, and this was the first year since Lisa's death that he genuinely felt like celebrating instead of going through the motions.

Vanessa knew all about the emotional ups and downs that certain holidays can trigger. As a young child, she had loved watching the animated television special *A Charlie Brown Christmas*. Every year her mother gave her freshly baked cookies and a glass of milk to enjoy while watching the cast of characters define the true meaning of Christmas. And, of course, while that tradition had ended decades ago, the sweet memory of it resurfaced the Christmas after her parents' passing. Vanessa had turned on the television one evening, and the special was playing. Instantly, the warm memories of her mother and baked cookies came to mind, practically crumbling her spirit.

In the bereavement counseling classes that had ended last week, Regina had reminded all of them that it was fine to feel whatever you feel during the holiday season, including sadness. She had told them to be gentle with themselves and to do only what was good for their spirit. It was sound advice that Vanessa planned to use—not just during the holidays but every day.

"Good morning, Nicole," Vanessa said stepping into the warmth of Elliott's home, carrying several bags of scrapbooking materials.

"Hi, Vanessa!" Nicole smiled, holding the door open for her. Taking one of the bags, she peeked inside. "Wow, this is awesome!"

"I thought you might like these bright colors. Have you picked out the pictures of your mom you want to include in the book?"

"Yep, and Dad helped me. But I think looking at the pictures made him sad."

Vanessa took off her coat and hung it in the hall closet. "Where is your dad?"

"In his office. He had a business call to make."

Walking into the dining room, Vanessa stopped in her tracks at the sight of so many photos of Lisa. They covered half of the dining room table. Cringing inwardly, she wondered if this had been such a good idea after all. But now was not the time to turn back. After taking a deep breath and summoning up a cheerful smile, she turned to Nicole. "Nicole, honey, let's get started. We're going to have a creative day!"

The two emptied the bags, organizing all the supplies on the table. Vanessa explained how to use the various colorful items to make a creative scrapbook. Once she was sure Nicole had the swing of it, she turned the reins over to her to design the book in her own personal style.

With Nicole engrossed, working her magic with stickers and glue, Vanessa eased into a chair at the end of the table to look at the photos. There were many of Lisa as a young girl, but the photos Vanessa especially zoomed in on were the ones of Lisa with Elliott—on their wedding day and later with their newly born baby girl, Nicole. They looked good together and extremely happy, celebrating holidays and enjoying vacations. For Vanessa, it felt surreal to see photos of the man she was now in love with clearly in love with another woman. As she continued flipping through the pictures, she came across some with Lisa looking weaker, thinner, and smiling a little less—photos taken during her battle with breast cancer.

Feeling a wave of sadness about to wash over her, Vanessa stood and excused herself. "I'll be back in a minute, Nicole. I just need to check on your dad."

"Okay—but before you go—how does this look?" She held up a scrapbook page with a photo of her with her mother in matching bathing suits, walking along the shores of a beach. Nicole appeared to be around three years old. Admiring the seashell stickers that Nicole had placed around the page, Vanessa smiled, giving her thumbs-up approval before walking down the hall to Elliott's office.

With her ear to the closed door, Vanessa took a deep breath and tapped softly.

"It's unlocked, come on in."

"Hey, are you all right?" Vanessa asked softly, stepping into the office and closing the door behind her. "I miss you out there," she said, nodding her head in the direction of the dining room. "I hope this scrapbook project isn't upsetting you."

Elliott smiled at Vanessa but didn't answer. He looked tired. He had been so concerned about Nicole's reaction to the scrapbooking project that he had never considered the emotional impact it might have on him to wade through all those photos of Lisa. The photos took him back in time, overwhelming him a bit.

Vanessa knew what Elliott needed, because she needed it, too. Taking a couple of steps toward him, he surprised her by getting up and meeting her half way. For several long minutes nothing was said as they embraced, holding on tightly to each other.

"I'm much better now that you're here," he finally said. Slowly releasing each other, he asked, "How do you think Nicole's doing?"

"I think she's fine. Right now she's caught up in the creative process, she's not reflecting on her loss. In my opinion, that's good."

Agreeing, Elliott nodded. "After Lisa passed, I talked quite a bit about her with Nicole. But to tell you the truth, I haven't talked too much about Lisa recently."

Vanessa looked at Elliott intently. "Is that because of me?"

Elliott was quiet, carefully considering Vanessa's question. After a couple of moments, he said, "Yeah, sweetie, it's because of you. Anyone can see how crazy Nicole is about you, and I want her to freely feel that way without thinking she's being disloyal to Lisa's memory."

"What makes you think she would feel disloyal?"

Exhaling, Elliott said, "Not long after we started dating, she asked me if I thought her mom would be mad at her if she likes you. Of course, I told her that her mom would be *happy* to have her like someone who's so nice to her. She seemed to really like that answer, but sometimes I sense that she still struggles with how she's supposed to feel about seeing me move on and fall in love again."

"You know what I'd like?"

Raising his brow, Elliott asked, "What's that?"

Reaching up and caressing the side of Elliott's face, Vanessa said. "I'd like for you to feel comfortable talking about Lisa with me—and with Nicole—without thinking that it'll hurt either one of us. It's natural for Lisa to be in your heart. She was your first love, your wife, and the mother of your child. And yet, all of that takes nothing away from what we have and feel for each other. You and Nicole mean everything to me and together we'll just sort through all of these shifting emotions."

Elliott pulled Vanessa closer in his arms and smiled. "When I think I can't possibly love you more than I already do, you give me new reasons." After kissing her, he said, "I like how wise you've become on the subject of grief."

Vanessa smiled. "Yeah, I guess I'm making some progress, thanks to you and my four new friends from my grief counseling group. Even though the course is over, we're going to continue meeting for a while—perhaps on a quarterly schedule for dinner and conversation. I volunteered to organize the first dinner in March."

Elliott smiled. "Why am I not surprised?" he teased taking her by the hand. "Now, let's go out here and check on our girl and see how she's doing."

A couple of hours later, Nicole finished her special scrapbook. Vanessa and Elliott helped her neatly stack the remaining loose photos of Lisa in a vintage-looking treasure box that Vanessa had brought over for Nicole to store photos and keepsakes. The remaining scrapbook material was stored away so that Nicole could create other memory books later on.

With dinner and movie plans in place with Elliott for later in the evening, Vanessa prepared to go home and get ready for their date. As she reached for her coat, Nicole ran over to her and hugged her tightly around the waist.

"Thanks so much for helping me!" Nicole said, holding on to Vanessa.

"Nicole, you're welcome," Vanessa said, hugging her back. "I hope you know how special you are to me."

"I do," she said, looking up at Vanessa. "And I feel the same about you."

Chapter 19

Christmas Day arrived, bringing with it gray skies and below-freezing temps. But inside Elliott's holiday-decorated home, the temperature was wonderfully warm. Elliott's parents had arrived yesterday from New Jersey, and two of his male cousins, who lived in the DC metropolitan area, had come by with their wives to spend the day and have dinner. Elliott's sister, Evelyn, had left this morning to travel with Paul and Sonya to visit Paul's family in Philadelphia, Pennsylvania.

Elliott's parents were thrilled to spend Christmas Eve with Nicole, while Elliott and Vanessa enjoyed a comfy evening at her joyfully-decorated home. After eating a delicious supper that they'd made together, they put on their heavy coats and took a brisk walk through her neighborhood, checking out all of the holiday decorations. Later, after an enjoyable Skype video call with Mike and Rita, they'd cuddled on her couch in front of a cozy fire, watching *The Preacher's Wife* holiday movie. Afterward, they exchanged gifts. Vanessa happily opened a box containing a stunning black opal pendant crafted in 24-karat gold. It was a match to the dangle earrings he had given her for her birthday. And Elliott was equally happy with his gift of engraved black onyx cufflinks crafted in sterling silver. Vanessa had also surprised him with a power-oriented tennis racket that had caught his attention in a magazine a week earlier. Generous gifts aside, they were just overjoyed for quality time together.

But, today, it was Nicole's turn to be spoiled with gifts. Sitting on the carpeted floor in the living room—surrounded by family and a bundle of wrapped presents—Nicole eagerly opened one gift after the other.

Sitting on the couch beside Elliott, Vanessa watched Nicole with amazement. For a nine-year-old, she was such a polite and sociable child. *Just like her dad*, Vanessa thought, as she shifted her eyes to Elliott, who was smiling at

Nicole with pride. With each gift Nicole opened, she said to the giver of the gift something nice about the present: "I like the color of this blouse." "These slippers look warm."

After opening the last gift, her grandmother said, "Nicole, I think you may have missed a gift. What's that over there under the tree?"

Nicole flashed a smile, as she reached under the tree and picked up the package. Holding it close to her, she said, "Grandma, this is my special scrapbook. It's filled with photos of my mom. I put it under the tree this morning, so it would feel like she was here with us today."

Suddenly, the festive mood changed as her sweet and innocent sentiment hung in the air. Elliott's family looked surprised, thinking that Nicole's homage to her mother was sweet—but awkward with Vanessa in the room. Their eyes quickly bounced from Nicole to Vanessa to Elliott. His cousin, Eric, thought, *Nicole unintentionally just put her dad between two women.*

Elliott, also surprised, hoped it didn't register on his face as he rose from the couch. "Come here, baby girl," he said gently and with a tender smile. Nicole stepped forward, and he pulled her into his embrace. Looking around the room at everyone, Elliott said cheerfully, "The holidays are about being with family and that means remembering our loved ones in heaven. Lisa will always be in our hearts, and I love that Nicole is thinking about her today with this pretty scrapbook." Pausing a moment, he looked directly at Vanessa and said, "And I deeply appreciate that Vanessa, who makes me so unbelievably happy, came up with the idea for the scrapbook and guided Nicole in making it."

"Why, that's wonderful!" exclaimed Eric's wife, Coretta. And judging by the smiles on all the other faces, they agreed with her.

Looking up at Elliott from her seat on the couch, Vanessa felt a lump in her throat. *From the day we met, he has had my back—offering prayer, encouragement, and love.*

Nicole quickly added, "Vanessa bought all the supplies. And she helped me organize my mom's pictures."

"That's very sweet, dear," Mrs. Reeves said as she turned to look at Vanessa. Unlike the rest of Elliott's family, who were friendly and easily approachable, Mrs. Reeves' disposition was more like a slow-cooking pot. She didn't warm up quickly. She took her own sweet time sizing up people and—until a few moments ago—her opinion of Vanessa was still anybody's guess. They had met for the first time yesterday afternoon at Evelyn's home for a potluck lunch. Vanessa had attended, but was forced to leave early as she was helping her sorority sisters serve an afternoon lunch at a homeless shelter. Inwardly, Mrs. Reeves bristled at the way Vanessa had breezed in and out within an hour of meeting each other—even if it was for charitable reasons. She'd needed more time to size up Vanessa and determine her intentions toward Elliott and Nicole. The senior Mr. Reeves, however, had fallen under Vanessa's spell in five minutes.

"Nicole, let me see the book," Mrs. Reeves said, taking it from her granddaughter. Turning the pages, her face softened. "Oh, this is beautiful, sweetheart."

Smiling, Nicole excused herself and left the room, only to return seconds later carrying a package. "This gift is for you, Vanessa."

Surprised to see Nicole offering her a gift, Vanessa glanced at Elliott, who gave her a clueless expression. He didn't know anything about this particular gift. He looked curiously at Nicole. *My child is full of surprises today. Please God, whatever this is—let it be all right.*

"Nicole, should I open it now or later?"

"Please open it now!" Nicole said, her eyes shining.

When Vanessa removed the wrapping paper, she couldn't believe her eyes. And neither could Elliott. His daughter had made a scrapbook about Vanessa that was simply precious.

Deeply touched, Vanessa said, "Nicole, I love my book — thank you so much! Who helped you with the photos?"

"Aunt Evelyn helped, and so did Sonya. We went on the Internet and got some from your website." The majority of the photos showed Vanessa's skills as an event planner, but there were also snapshots that Evelyn had taken of Vanessa with Nicole—at the zoo, at a football game, on Halloween night, and just a few weeks ago on Thanksgiving Day.

Vanessa chuckled. "Well, you all have been busy! I'll thank Evelyn and Sonya when I see them in a couple of days."

Looking at Nicole with amusement, Elliott said, "You're full of surprises today. But I have a question for you."

"What's that, Daddy?"

Laughing, he lifted his arms and asked, "Can I get some love, too? Where's my scrapbook? I'm the one who's going to put you through college."

Everyone broke up laughing. Even Mrs. Reeves cracked a big smile—and held it while turning toward Vanessa. Elliot's mother was warming up. After all, if her granddaughter was scrapbooking about this woman after only a few months, then she'd better get to know her quickly!

Nicole pouted a little. "Daddy, you spoiled my surprise! You're getting your book on Valentine's Day."

Elliott embraced Nicole and tickled her. As she giggled, he said, "I love you—and I'm sorry for spoiling your surprise."

Turning around to his mother, Elliott extended his hand and she happily accepted it. Lifting her to her feet, he said joyfully, "My kitchen and oven has been getting a real workout since yesterday—Mama has been working her culinary magic! Aside from the turkey, she's prepared cornbread stuffing, sweet potatoes with pineapples and pecans, collard greens, and string beans."

"Daddy, don't forget the pumpkin pie," Nicole chimed in. "I helped Grandma make it this morning."

With everyone's admiration now on Mrs. Reeves, she chuckled and shrugged her shoulders. "Well, what can I say? I love to cook and spoil my family!" And then with a tease, she added, "But know this, you all are going to clean up that kitchen—*not me*! I'm going to sit down after dinner and put my feet up!"

Elliott laughed along with everyone else. "Mama, we love you and wouldn't have it any other way! Come on everybody, this is a joyful and blessed day. Let's say the grace and eat."

Walking toward the dining room with Vanessa at his side, Elliott smiled and thought, *Happy Birthday, Jesus! Thank you for being in the middle of all of these surprises.*

Chapter 20

The male chorus of Moses Baptist Church was ready to lift their voices and sing on this first Sunday morning in February. Dressed in black suits, white shirts, and red neckties, all sixty-five members were lined up in the rear of the church, looking mighty righteous while waiting for the morning service to start.

Elliott, who was standing among them, turned his head a bit, trying to locate Vanessa and Nicole. Spotting them in seats near the center aisle, he noticed that Nicole was chuckling at whatever Vanessa was whispering in her ear. *Those two are always up to something fun*, he thought, a wide smile on his face.

Minutes later, an elderly deacon stepped to the pulpit and rendered a spirited appeal to God for blessings and guidance. When he finished, the choir director nodded to the musicians, and they began to play the morning hymn. As the male chorus processed down the center aisle, singing loudly and harmoniously, worshippers stood up to receive them.

As Elliott passed by the pew where Vanessa and Nicole sat, he tilted his head to make eye contact with them. And they were ready for him, giving him a big smile and two thumbs up. With a playful wink, he returned the smile.

The lofty seats behind the pulpit offered the choir a full view of the congregation. From his seat, Elliott appreciated the view of Vanessa and Nicole clapping their hands and lightly swaying to the music. He chuckled inwardly looking at Nicole. She was a tad off beat in rhythm but pouring her heart into the morning hymn.

The worship service moved fluently with a responsive reading, a second hymn, and announcements, followed by tithes and offerings.

An hour into the service, it was now preaching time. The guest minister was a woman from Doswell, Virginia. Vanessa listened with interest as Reverend

Elizabeth Allen's calm and soothing voice filled the sanctuary. "It's my great honor to be with all of you this morning. And I promise I will not be before you too long on this lovely Sunday in the wintry month of February that our Lord has given us to enjoy!"

A loud chorus of Amen came from the deacons.

Smiling broadly, Reverend Allen said, "Thank you, deacons! Although I'm not sure if you said Amen because you're happy that I'm not going to preach long, or because you're happy the Lord has given us this day. But I'm just going to assume you're glad about both of those things."

Laughter filled the sanctuary.

Smiling, she said, "My brothers and sisters in Christ, I stopped by here this morning to remind you that despite all of the depressing and devastating things happening around us and to us, we must never give up on the miracle-working power of the precious gift of L-O-V-E. As Christians, we must strive to love and lift each other up, just as our Lord and Savior loves us and lifts us up through all of our circumstances."

Ample rounds of praise followed her comments.

"Love is fascinating, isn't it? We write about love and sing about love, just as we've been doing all morning with our hymns and chorus selections. We tear each other down over love and build each other up again because of love." Pausing a moment, she said, "The other day, I heard an old song on the radio that asked the question: What does love have to do with it? How many of you all remember it?"

A lot of hands went up throughout the congregation.

With a chuckle, Reverend Allen said, "Thank you, I knew I wasn't the only one back in the day enjoying the smooth tempo of that song."

The congregation responded with laughter.

Reverend Allen took a sip of water and said, "But seriously, my brothers and my sisters, after reflecting on that critical question, I stand before you this morning to tell you with 100 percent assurance that love has everything to do with it! No matter what the situation, love needs to be squarely in the center of it all. And if there's anybody who needs a shining example of love, look no further than our Lord and Savior, Jesus, for he is the greatest love we'll ever know. And having the love of Jesus means we have everything!"

"Amen, Reverend!" replied the assistant pastor. A fresh chorus of praise flowed throughout the sanctuary.

Reverend Allen was preaching now, "The apostle Paul, a great man and fervent messenger of the gospel of Jesus Christ, was a bona fide master teacher on the subject of love. When the leaders of the Corinthian church found their congregations struggling with various problems, they turned to Paul. They knew he would tell them that love should always guide their behavior. Paul wrote them an extraordinary letter offering his perspective on being obedient to Christ, and working for unity and love in the church. In the book of First Corinthians, it's in the thirteenth chapter that Paul declares love is far greater than faith and hope. And that sincere devotion to God and love for each other exceeds all other gifts in the world. Please always remember, my brothers and sisters, that when all of what we have diminishes, love is the one thing that will continue."

With many people in the congregation applauding, the preacher vigorously continued, "Sadly, I believe that society, over time, has weakened the definition of love because we throw the word around without even thinking about what it truly means. But Paul makes it plain the type of love we must strive to have in our hearts. Let's open the Bible and read what it says..."

Turning to look at Vanessa, Nicole whispered, "There's a lot to say about love, isn't there?"

Smiling at her, Vanessa replied, "Yes, there is, Nicole. Love is everything!"

"Just so you know—I love you! And so does my dad, because he told me so."

Surprised by Nicole's loving statement, Vanessa's heart swelled with affection. Looking into Nicole's eyes, she said, "Well, sweetheart, I hope you know that I love you and your dad."

Nicole knew it, inching closer and nestling comfortably under Vanessa's right arm.

As the minister continued preaching the merits of love, Elliott noticed Vanessa's head slightly bowed. Nicole was snuggled under her arm, listening attentively to the preacher. He wondered what Vanessa was thinking. Suddenly, she lifted her head, wiping away joyful tears forming in the corner of her eyes.

The minister continued preaching, her tone softer now, "Church, I know it's not easy to always love the way Paul instructs us to do. We live in a world full of people with shamefully horrible behavior, and the idea of loving them seems absurd when we don't even *like* them. But, you see, love is supposed to rise above what we like or what we want. Love is about self-sacrifice and having compassion for everybody, and recognizing that the person who deserves our love the least is the one who needs it the most."

"Amen," said the congregation.

"In all of your relationships, give your very best at all times. When it comes to romantic love, many of us are still waiting for the right one to come along. In fact, I'm still waiting for the right man and trusting that God's going to work it out for me. But if you already have someone special and believe that God has brought you together, I urge you to celebrate your love and to protect it. Be good to each other. Love each other as if there's no tomorrow. Love each other with a sense of urgency."

"*Amen!*" Elliott declared to himself.

It was 2 p.m. that afternoon, and Nicole was on a critical mission. Clearly inspired by the numerous times she had heard the word "love" in this morning's sermon, she was seated at Vanessa's kitchen table, going through the Bible searching for more verses referencing love.

"Nicole, how many have you found so far?" Vanessa asked, as she spooned her homemade sweet pepper sauce over the turkey meatloaf she was preparing for their Sunday dinner.

"I've found thirty, but there must be more; after all, this is the Bible!"

Vanessa laughed. "Yes, you can be certain there are a lot more to find."

"What are you two talking about?" Elliott asked as he walked into the kitchen carrying a white pie-shaped box. He was just now arriving at Vanessa's after running an errand following the morning service. Vanessa was at the kitchen counter, inspecting her meatloaf. Giving Vanessa a quick kiss on the cheek, Elliott placed the white box on the far side of the counter.

"Daddy, I want to know how many scriptures there are with the word "love" in them. I want to look them all up and read them."

Removing his suit jacket and draping it across the back of the kitchen chair, Elliott smiled. "You usually fall asleep and snore during preaching time, so I'm glad today's sermon kept you awake and inspired you to read the Bible."

Giggling, Nicole said, "Daddy, I do not snore."

Elliott smiled and said, "If you say so. Hey, while you have the Bible open, see if there's a scripture that says love means never being away from those you love for more than three days."

"Huh?" Nicole asked.

Playfully rolling her eyes at Elliott, Vanessa said, "Don't pay your dad any attention. He's not happy with me because I have some business travel coming up, and I'll be away from you guys for six days."

"Six days!" Nicole exclaimed, her eyes widening. "When were you going to tell me?"

Vanessa chuckled as she placed the meatloaf back in the oven to warm the sweet pepper sauce. "You two make six short days sound like six long weeks." Turning to Nicole, she said, "I was going to tell *you* today."

Looking concerned, Nicole asked, "When do you leave? And where are you going?"

Surprised by Nicole's panicky reaction and her questions, Vanessa smiled at her and then said jokingly, "Young lady, I guess when you grow up you'll be a lawyer like your daddy, because you certainly can ask a lot of questions."

Blushing, Nicole said, "Sorry, Vanessa, I just don't want you to leave us."

Vanessa walked over and hugged Nicole. "Sweetie, believe me, I don't want to leave you or your dad, but on occasion I do have to travel for business. I'm taking the train to Connecticut next Sunday—and I'm excited about it because I'll be working on a new project that'll help grow my consulting business." Pausing, she leaned down and made direct eye contact with Nicole. "But beware, young lady, because the minute I get back, I'm giving all my attention to you and your dad!"

Nicole smiled brightly. "Okay, just hurry back!"

Elliott laughed. "I agree with my daughter."

Vanessa, smiling lovingly at both of them, playfully tapped Nicole's shoulder and said, "Now, please go wash your hands and then come help me set the table in the dining room. I don't know about you, but I'm hungry and ready to eat!"

"I'm hungry, too!" Nicole said. Turning to leave the kitchen, she spotted the white box on the counter. Stopping in her tracks, she asked, "Daddy, what's in the box?"

Raising her eyebrows, Vanessa asked, "Yeah, honey, what's in the box?"

With Vanessa and Nicole standing before him and waiting for an answer, Elliott thought, *I wanted this to wait until after dinner, but I guess now is as good a time as any.* Taking a deep breath, he walked over to the counter, picking up the white box. Turning and facing Vanessa, his expression grew serious. His eyes gleamed as he stared at her. "Sweetie, this is for you."

Just for me? Vanessa accepted the box from Elliott and lifted the lid. Stunned at what she saw, she looked up at him and then back down at the box. *Is this for real?*

Elliott eased the box from her tight grip and placed it on the table. Taking both of her hands, he went down on one knee. Looking up in Vanessa's eyes, which were filling with tears, Elliott said in a voice thick with emotion, "Vanessa Grace Dennison, will you please marry me?"

Vanessa and Elliott talked all the time about the future—sharing their hopes and dreams alike—each believing that they would one day soon settle down together. And while Vanessa had never imagined that Elliott would propose to her today, it didn't stop her from being ready with an answer.

Now, holding tightly to Elliott's hands, Vanessa also went down on one knee and, with tears streaming down her face, whispered, "Elliott Jason Reeves, yes, I will marry you!"

Nicole, thrilled to witness all of this happiness going on in front of her, grinned from ear to ear. She quietly went to the table and lifted the lid on the box. Inside was a large heart-shaped oatmeal cookie with white frosting writing: "Will You Marry Me?" Picking up the Bible, and tiptoeing from the kitchen, she smiled brightly. *I think Daddy and Vanessa need a minute alone.*

"I love you so much!" Elliott said, rising to his feet and pulling Vanessa up with him. His eyes were wet with tears. Wrapping his arms around her as she wiped away her tears, he said, "I was waiting until Valentine's Day to ask you to marry me. But after the minister reminded us all today to love each other like there is no tomorrow and with a sense of urgency, something moved in my spirit and I knew I had to ask you *today* to be my wife."

"Elliott, you're an amazing man, and I'm so grateful to God for bringing us together." Turning and looking at the box, she said, "And I love my cookie proposal!"

Laughing, he said, "Well, it's the only creative thing I could think of at the moment. But in some ways it's appropriate since the first thing we shared together was an oatmeal cookie at a Broadway play."

"That's right." She smiled brightly, remembering that night at the theater.

Leaning into each other's arms, they sealed their engagement with a tender kiss. When they broke from their embrace, Elliott said, "I want to put a beautiful engagement ring on your finger, but I want you to pick it out. And after we get the ring, let's gather our family and friends to celebrate with a party."

"I'd love a party, but we have to set a date because that's the first question everyone will ask us."

Elliott smiled. "Can I convince you to be a June bride?"

Vanessa said with excitement, "Honey, that's in four months!" Already her mind was thinking of the preparation they would need to do before getting married. Remembering how much she loves the fall season, she asked, "How about an autumn wedding in late September or early October? The extra months will give us time to plan a gorgeous wedding! And time to figure out everything else in our lives that we'll need to merge either before or after we get married." Thinking of her home in Richmond, she laughed and said, "Between us, we'll have three homes. We've got a lot of decisions to make!"

Elliott wanted to marry Vanessa sooner rather than later. But he knew she was right about putting a plan in place and getting organized. He nodded in agreement. "Early autumn it is, my love. But not any later—promise me!"

"I promise you and I love you! We'll get the calendar out tonight and circle a date," she said, reaching up to him and sealing her promise with a kiss.

Looking at Vanessa thoughtfully, Elliott asked, "How would you feel about getting married in Manhattan? It's where we met, and where you and your parents enjoyed good times together. I'm sure we can find the perfect venue to have a beautiful wedding."

Blinking back a fresh stream of tears, Vanessa said, "Honey, I love the idea!" Hugging him tightly, she added, "Let's do it—Manhattan, here we come!"

Hurrying back into the kitchen carrying the Bible, Nicole said with excitement, "I found a scripture we could read at the wedding! It paints a pretty picture of love. Do you want to hear it?"

Smiling brightly at his precious daughter, Elliott said, "Baby girl, of course we want to hear it, but the prettiest picture of love is the three of us together!" And with that said, Elliott and Vanessa both reached for Nicole, pulling her into their loving embrace.

About the Author

Elsie Hillman-Gordon holds a BA in English from Livingstone College, and has completed executive graduate work in marketing at Strayer University. She lives with her husband in Washington, DC.

A life member of Alpha Kappa Alpha Sorority, Inc., Elsie stays busy in her free time supporting community outreach projects sponsored through her sorority. She does volunteer work with her church and nonprofit organizations. And recently, has also extended her helping hand through writing. Her debut book, *Love Is Everything*, is a work of fiction, although it's sure to serve as a source of inspiration to countless hearts in need of healing.

Elsie welcomes readers to write her at: elsiehillmangordon@gmail.com.

Made in the USA
Charleston, SC
16 July 2014